# The Ugly Truth

## by

## Cheryel Hutton

**The Ugly Truth**

Cover Art by *Debbie Taylor*

The Wild Rose Press, Inc.
PO Box 708
Adams Basin, NY 14410-0708
Visit us at www.thewildrosepress.com

Publishing History
First Faery Rose Edition, 2013
Print ISBN 978-1-61217-854-7
Digital ISBN 978-1-61217-855-4

Published in the United States of America

**My camera was in my hand without conscious** thought. I clicked away for a moment, then exchanged the digital for my trusty thirty-five millimeter single lens reflex. Not only might the film catch something the pixels didn't, there would be a negative for proof. I even had enough time to fit a filter over the lens before the light/object zipped away toward the distant mountains. As I watched, whatever had visited the festival disappeared up and over the top of the highest peak.

"Holy crap," Maddie muttered.

I nodded. My sentiments exactly.

Only slowly did I realize the high-pitched sound was gone, replaced by an almost unearthly quiet. Little by little the murmur of voices began to grow louder. I looked at Maddie, and she looked at me, wide-eyed and just a bit pale. She turned to speak to her mother and I found myself looking back over my shoulder. Jake looked right at me.

His gaze met mine, and he mouthed, "Whoa."

I nodded, and he smiled. My heart leaped, and other parts of my body warmed and softened. The man was just too freaking good looking for my own good.

Then he looked away, and I turned back to the front. Music was again filling the air, and I leaned back and tried to relax. I noticed, though, I wasn't the only one who kept glancing upward. Apparently, a UFO wasn't usual even in Ugly Creek.

Thank goodness.

# Dedication

To my Mom,
wish you were here to enjoy this with me.
I miss you.

# Acknowledgements

Thank you to the
Chattanooga Area Romance Authors.
CARA rocks!

Chapter 1

Welcome Back, Ugly Grads!

I gaped up at the banner draped across the front of Ugly Creek High School gymnasium. How had I let myself get talked into coming to this thing? I needed my head examined, that was for sure.

Me? I'm Stephie, and somebody else's reunion is *so* not my idea of a fun time.

"Welcome to the reunion." A guy with blond hair and wire-framed glasses smiled toward me. The long table he stood behind was covered with nametags, flyers, and programs.

I turned to my companion, only to find she wasn't there. "Excuse me a minute," I said to the handsome gatekeeper, and headed back to the big double doors. She was there, cowering near the entrance.

"Come on, Maddie. This is your gig. I'm only riding shotgun." I tugged on her arm, and she literally dragged her feet as she slowly walked into the gym.

"I'm going to throw up."

I resisted the urge to roll my eyes. Barely. "No, you're not. You'll be fine."

"I'm serious."

I caught sight of Maddie's face and decided to rethink the situation. I figured the green tint of her skin was due to the bad lighting, but what if I was wrong? "Take deep breaths," I told her, for lack of any other useful advice.

"Oh, Stephie! It looks exactly like it did ten years ago."

I looked more closely and realized there was a hint of wildness in those big blue eyes of hers. If she got hysterical, I had an obligation to slap her to calm her down, right? Then again, that might not be such a good idea—she had an awesome right hook.

"All school gyms look alike," I told my green-around-the-gills friend. Why do they say that anyway? It's not like people actually have gills.

Maddie pointed to a sign stenciled on the back wall in huge green and black letters, *Ugly Creek High School, home of the Gators.* Below it, a humongous green alligator was drooling to devour the other team. Any other team.

"The lettering is the same; the floor is the same; the smell is the same." Her eyes glistened and she sniffled. "Everything is exactly the same. It's almost like there was never a fire."

I put a hand on her shoulder. I'd never thought of Maddie as anything but strong and determined, but she seemed on the verge of a meltdown. "I'm going to get you through this week of high-school-reunion-slash-Big Foot-Festival." I would too. I owed her big time.

"I really don't think I can do this."

"Yes, you can." Personally, I was sure envy-inducing Madison, tall, blonde, self-assured woman with a great fashion sense—in other words, the opposite of not-envy-inducing me—would be fine in any situation.

She shook her head. "I'm not so sure."

I realized I had to do something before she lost it.

The way I saw it, my options were to slap her, distract her, or throw her over my shoulder and head for the door. Since slapping her did seem a little mean, and since I'm only five-two, I knew I'd never get her Amazonian bod to the door. Distraction seemed the best choice.

"When do I get to meet a Sasquatch?" I asked, eyes innocent, grin sternly quashed.

Maddie groaned. "How many times have I told you? The Big Foot Festival was named after the town founder."

"They seriously named a festival after the guy's big feet? Sounds insulting to me." Distracting her was working. Yay for me.

"His feet were *huge*, okay?" There was exasperation in her voice.

I pretended to think a moment. "I bet he had a tiny car." I leaned closer. "A big red nose, a white face, and a multicolor wig."

She didn't look green anymore. Now her face was Irritation Strawberry.

"I told you, Stephanova," she said, her voice quiet, "There are no legendary creatures in Ugly Creek."

By this time, I'd managed to pull her over to the table again. Me, the girl with the crazy brown hair and the sundress without a designer tag, had managed to get my fashion-conscious friend to the check-in. Whew, crisis averted.

"Maddie?" the guy with glasses asked, though it was obvious he knew her. "How are you?"

"Steve, hi! I'm fine. How are you?"

Then they leaned across the table to hug. I guess she was all better now. He gave her a nametag, while

3

they talked rapidly about things I knew nothing about—and didn't want to. He shoved a yellow "visitor" tag my way, along with a black marker. "Would you mind?"

He asked nicely and smiled, so I wrote "Stephie" on the tag and hung it around my neck. My name is really Buffy Stephanova, but that's nobody's business but mine. I'm not a vampire slayer, or a bitchy rich girl.

"Maddie!" a loud, high-pitched voice squealed.

"Liza!" Madison shrieked and took off toward the squeal.

My ears rang as I watched as Madison and a slightly shorter blonde grabbed each other and proceeded to shriek, squeal, and jump up and down. They reminded me of two odd, and loud, birds.

I aimed my camera toward them and shot some pics for my friend. And yeah, my amusement.

The squealers turned toward me, and I used my Nikon to hide the wide-eyed-oh-my-God-they're-headed-this-way expression. Luckily, as a photojournalist, I'm used to operating in the line of fire.

Still, dodging a livid senator or celebrity I did all the time. The closer Maddie and her friend got, the more this felt like strip poker. And I was losing.

I used every tactic I'd ever learned as a terminally shy, stumbling-through-her-career photojournalist, and by the time Maddie and her friend got to me, the compulsion to race out of there and back to D.C. had lessened to heart-pounding apprehension.

I lowered my camera and hoped I didn't blow chunks right there in the middle of the Ugly Creek High School's ten year anniversary meet and greet.

Why was it again I had felt the need to go to somebody else's reunion?

"Stephie, this is my good friend Liza. Liza, this is my also good friend, coworker, and roommate from D.C., Stephie."

"It's nice to meet you, Stephie. Every time Maddie writes or calls she mentions you." She tipped her head to one side as she eyed my yellow visitor tag. "Odd, she's never mentioned your last name."

And then I remembered. I was there to support my best friend and reliable confidant, Madison Clark. I smiled her way and she gave a little wink to let me know she knew I knew she had kept quiet, and this Liza wasn't on any need-to-know list.

"So what is your last name?" Liza asked.

Oh great, she's pushy. Kind of like Maddie. Figures. Oh, what the hell? "Stephanova."

"So...Stephie is short for Stephanova?"

And quick with the connections. Again like Maddie. I was irritated, but I couldn't help but admire this chick. "Yep."

Liza leaned her head to one side. "What's your first name?"

Okay, game over. I opened my mouth to tell her it was none of her damn business—in a polite way, of course—but I didn't get the chance.

"Nobody knows," Maddie said. "Rumor has it a couple of people found out, but we don't know for sure because they mysteriously disappeared."

Liza snorted, but didn't push the issue. "Maddie tells me you're a photojournalist."

"Yeah, we both work at *Capitol Spy Weekly*," I felt a familiar twinge when I said the name. Just because it was a D.C. tabloid didn't change the fact that it was, in fact, a tabloid.

"Do you work together, doing the reporter and photographer thing?" Liza asked.

"When we're lucky," Madison said. "And we have a blast when we do."

Before we could get into the talking about the job section of our conversation, the blond guy from the welcome table walked up and draped an arm around Liza.

Liza turned an admiring face up to him while sparks flew around the room. She still had a spellbound gaze when she said, "Stephie, this is my awesome husband, Steve."

I held out my hand, and he gave it a shake. "Nice to formally meet you," I said.

"Same here."

Maddie giggled. "Oh, I see Johnny Bright over there, and I do believe he has the worst comb-over in the history of the world."

Liza slowly pulled herself away from her man. "Let's go check him out."

"Wanna come?" Maddie asked me.

To see an ugly comb-over on a guy I don't know and don't want to know? "I don't think so. You two go on."

Liza and Maddie headed toward the eleventh wonder of the high school reunion world, leaning close and giggling like the teenagers they were ten years ago.

"Madison is all Liza's talked about for months."

I turned to the nametag guy, who still stood near me. As I moved, I caught sight of his nametag. Steve Zapata.

I recognized the name, and immediately shoved my size-seven-Italian-made-sandals-that-I'd-discovered-at-a-thrift-store into my overanxious mouth. "You're 'Shoe'."

Had I really just said that? I did the whole wishing I could go through the floor, the ground, maybe check out China. "Oh, God, I'm so sorry! I don't know why I said that."

Steve chuckled, while my face cooked in its own heat. "It's okay. I'm quite sure Maddie has told you all about me, and how I got my nickname."

"She said it was in Spanish class. Zapata, *zapato*."

He used one finger to nudge wire-frame glasses up his nose. "Close enough to the word for 'shoe' to be funny to Maddie, Liza, and approximately three hundred of our closest friends."

"I guess I never really got that you were the guy who married Liza."

He gazed across the big room toward Liza with a little smile of contentment and an admiring expression of his own. "Yep, I'm the lucky man."

The love I saw in his eyes gave me the warm fuzzies. It also, I am ashamed to admit, sent a small dose of jealousy through me. I wanted a man to look at me like that. Ridiculous, I know, but sometimes I get these romance novel ideas. Like that kind of stuff ever happens in real life. But then, the way Steve looked at Liza...

I clicked off a couple of shots, both to catch the moment and to cover the pathetic longing expression I feared covered my face. I'd embarrassed myself quite enough for one reunion.

"Hey, Steve," a male voice said. "How're you doing?"

Something about the resonant baritone played

tingles of a happy song up and down my spine. I looked toward the source of the remarkable voice, and damn near dropped my camera. Handsome. Sexy. Dark. Well-built. With a smile that could knock a girl off her sandals and all the way into the realm of lusty infatuation.

"Jake, old man," Steve said. "Glad you came out."

"Figured I might as well make an appearance, prove I'm still breathing."

His gaze caught mine, and I swear I heard birds singing. Then he grinned. Full lips, straight teeth, the cutest little dimple near one side of his wonderful mouth. I thought I was gonna melt.

"Hi, I'm Jake."

He's talking to me. Wake up, self, he's talking to me! "I'm Stephie," I managed, as I stuck out my hand.

He nodded to my yellow, visitor's, nametag. "So, you're here with somebody."

I nodded. "A friend."

He narrowed those dark, sexy eyes of his. "Boyfriend?"

I gave him my very best smile. "No. I'm here with Madison Clark. She's right over there."

I was still pointing when I looked back at him. He was staring toward Maddie with an expression of long-simmering-pissed-off-ishness. Great. Perfect Guy and my best friend had a history. And just when I was beginning to think this trip had potential. I probably should just keep my mouth shut, but curiosity was tugging at my sleeve. Besides, maybe it wasn't as bad as I thought. "So, you know her?"

"Yes." He stared for a moment longer. Then he looked at me, and there was regret in his eyes. "It was nice meeting you, Stephie. Later, Steve." Then he turned and headed toward the other side of the room as if something was chasing him.

Disappointment filled my insides and weighed me down. I wanted him back. Sigh.

"I'm surprised Maddie didn't tell you about Jake." Steve was staring in the direction Jake had gone.

"She actually doesn't talk much about the past," I told him, still staring after Handsome.

"Makes sense, I guess."

I had to know. Didn't want to, but had to. "Were they an item, Jake and Madison?"

He shrugged. "Not really."

My curiosity started to poke me in the belly. "They had some kind of falling out?"

He searched my face for a moment. "She really hasn't said anything?"

"Nothing. Honest."

"Jake was hurt in the fire." He frowned then. "You do know about the fire, right?"

"Prom night, in the gym, it was the night Maddie's dad died." I glanced toward my gorgeous friend. She'd never gotten over that night, and I was pretty sure she never would.

"That's the one. Jake got hurt pretty badly."

He stopped, and my curiosity jumped up and down. "And?" I prompted.

"You need to ask Maddie," he whispered.

I looked up to see Madison and Liza coming our way. Dang, things were just getting interesting.

While Maddie and her friend babbled about people I'd never heard of, I wondered what Steve had been hinting at. My always inquiring mind screamed at me to find out. Due to the combination of reunion and festival, Maddie and I planned to be here a week. By the time I returned to D.C., I intended to know the whole, sordid story. Besides, what else did I have to do in a little town like Ugly Creek, play fetch with alligators? Wait a minute, Tennessee is landlocked. There are no gators here. What the heck did alligators have to do with anything? Weird place.

A few minutes later Maddie and Liza took off to make fun of more of their fellow reunion-goers. Soon thereafter, Steve took off to talk to some of his friends. I was left alone to contemplate what the hell I was doing at a high school reunion that wasn't even mine, in the midst of a Big Foot Festival in a place that apparently didn't have Sasquatch, Bigfoot, Yeti, or even fake-human-in-a-suit creatures. How not fun was that?

There were, however, a lot of people in the building. Did I mention I'm not fond of large groups of anything, especially people?

With a huge, self-pitying sigh, I looked around for something to distract my nerves. Metal tables and chairs were scattered throughout the huge, blue tarp-covered floor, except for a raised area, with a microphone—a bad indication of boring speeches yet to come.

A thought came to me out of nowhere. When Maddie denied there were legendary creatures in Ugly Creek, she hadn't looked at me. In fact, two months ago, when she asked me to come with her, she had brushed off the name of the festival. Wouldn't talk about it. Hmm, maybe there was something she wasn't telling me. Maybe there were Bigfoot creatures in these parts. Maybe I could do some exploring.

Or maybe I was trying to find something to think about besides how out of place I felt at another person's high school reunion.

"Wasn't Mr. Blackwood's history class the pits?"

I looked toward the speaker, who was standing so close I could smell his expensive cologne.

The man's pinstripe gray, moderately expensive suit fit tight around his beach ball middle. His sparse brown hair was cut in a flattering style. He moved even closer, and I stepped back to get him out of my personal space. "I wouldn't know," I told him.

He chuckled. "Oh come on, I remember you from third period."

I edged back a bit, always better to keep your distance from a potentially unbalanced person no matter how good looking he was. "Sorry, you have me confused with someone else."

"Blackwood was a real pain," he said, as if I hadn't uttered a syllable. "Making us do all kinds of extra work."

*Blackwood.* "Is this teacher related to Jake Blackwood?"

The man's expression went from smile to suspicion without passing go. "You weren't in my class, were you?"

What do you know, there were a couple of brain cells in there. "No, I wasn't."

"So, how do you know Blackwood?"

I had him on the defensive. I swallowed back the threatening grin. "I told you, I wasn't in your class. How could I know this Mr. Blackwood?"

His nostrils flared in obvious frustration. "*Jake*

Blackwood."

I gave him my best wide-eyed stare. "That's the name of the teacher?"

The man's nostrils flared even wider, which was saying something.

"Butch, buddy. Are you bothering this nice lady?"

The voice startled Wide Nostrils. He took a step back before he turned and glared at Jake. "I'm not your buddy."

Jake didn't even blink; he just stared at the other man.

Butch snorted through his wide nostrils then turned and walked away.

A shiver of lingering annoyance moved through me, but was pushed away by the handsome man beside me. "Thank you for the rescue."

"No problem."

I felt a tingle in response to the twinkle in his eyes. I hadn't seen the right side of his face before, but now it was obvious that under the five o'clock shadow was a wide, flat scar. I realized I was staring when he put his fingers against it.

"I was in an accident."

My hand moved in the direction of his face, and I put it back down by my side where it belonged. "It looks good on you."

He stared at me for a moment, as if he thought I might be making fun of him. My sincerity must have come through, because he let out a quick, wry laugh. "I'm glad you like it."

"I'm sorry for the pain you must have gone through to get your scar, but it gives you a rugged look." I did touch his face then, with the tips of my fingers. "It's quite sexy."

"Sexy, huh?"

His eyes had gone from brown to black, and I felt an answering tingle deep inside my body. My breathing kicked up a notch, my heart banged hard against my ribs, I swallowed convulsively against the drying of my mouth. My hand moved again, toward the alien topography of his cheek. I could almost feel my lips pressing gently against the hard stubble covering the soft, flat reminder of what must have been a horrible experience.

Thinking of the fire reminded me of why I was in Ugly Creek—for the friend who had saved my job and sanity—and I dropped my hand to my side. "Yes, it's sexy."

"Thank you," he whispered.

I heard a high-pitched giggle, and when I looked in that direction, I saw Maddie and Liza heading my way. I instinctively glanced toward Jake, only to find he'd vanished. For the best, I guess. All I needed was to be caught in the middle of a confrontation between my best friend and the best thing this flea-butt town had to offer. I sighed. Such is my life.

"Just standing there by herself, looking bored. That's Stephie for you."

"I wasn't just standing here," I told Maddie. "I was talking to some of your classmates and taking pictures." And talking to a guy who could give Hugh Jackman a run for the money.

"Yeah, yeah, whatever. Let's go have some fun." She grabbed my arm.

"I'm fine right here." I'd rather stand here and see if this Jake dude came back, but Madison was persistent, and strong. So I finally gave in.

I spent the next eternity—I mean hour—meeting unremarkable people I could not have cared less about. There were some highlights, like an overly dramatic recreation of Jimmy, Ugly Creek High football's best wide receiver ever, looking directly into the unblinking male English teacher's eyes and reciting the poem "How Do I Love Thee, Let Me Count the Ways." I wasn't sure any amount of extra credit would be worth that kind of humiliation.

And then it was time for the boring speeches.

"Welcome to The Ugly Creek Big Foot Festival and our ten year high school reunion," said an average-looking, average-height man in a light brown suit that matched his light brown hair and light brown eyeglass frames. "For the benefit of the visitors and those with amnesia, I'll introduce myself. I'm Roy Palmer, class president, head of the reunion committee, and the owner of The Arcane Restaurant and Mystical Supply Shop. I'd like to invite y'all to come on down, and to encourage you, I'm offering a free tarot reading by our resident psychic, Connie Malone. All you have to do is show your nametag from this reunion and tell 'em what you want."

While he was babbling, the three of us settled at one of the tables scattered over the floor. Steve joined us there, sat next to his wife and smiled toward her with an expression of happiness that kicked me in the jealous bone.

The class president continued, "As I hope you know, because of the horrific tragedy of ten years ago, our class voted to expand and reschedule our reunion so we would be gathering during the week of the annual

Big Foot Festival. Our reunion committee and the city council worked together to make this week a very special one. The theme for this week is 'Heroes'. And it's a theme chosen by, and especially suited to, our class. Because it was one man, one hero, who ten years ago, paid the ultimate price in an effort to save members of our class."

I looked over at Maddie, and my heart twisted. This was why I was here, I reminded myself, to support her through what was sure to be an agonizing experience. I'm not sure I'd have had the guts to come and face the loss all over again. But if I had, she would come with me, of that I was sure.

"No one knows exactly how the fire started, though there is no shortage of theories. What we do know, is how quickly the flames spread through the gym where the prom was in full swing. Before we knew what was happening, the smoke was so thick it was impossible to see. Sometimes, if I listen carefully, I almost believe I can still hear the screams."

He paused, and I strained to hear the residual echo of what must have been a hellish night.

"Virgil Clark and his fellow firemen saved many of us from the inferno," he continued, his voice tight, and the index cards in his hands trembling. "All of them acted with skill and bravery, but Mr. Clark gave his very life to save others. It is in his memory that both the reunion and the festival are dedicated."

He stepped down, and applause filled the room. I wasn't paying attention, though, because I was focused on Madison. Tears filled her eyes and overflowed onto her cheeks. "Daddy," she whispered, as she wiped at her face. I put my hand on her arm, but the gesture felt so inadequate it seemed hardly worth it. I caught Liza's expression out of the corner of my eye, and she looked just about how I felt. We could be there for Maddie, but we couldn't protect her from the pain this week was going to cause. Tears stung my own eyes as I thought about my own father. Not taken by a disaster like Maddie's, my father just walked away one day and never came back. Was it worse not to know if your dad ever even loved you?

As I forced my mind back to the event, I heard the call for volunteers to help out during the week-long festival, and I had a bout of nostalgia as a wave of people washed toward the sign-up table. Small town people have big hearts.

Dang, what was wrong with me? I shoved the thought into the long-forgotten recesses of my mind. As I turned back toward my friend, I saw Jake across the room. He stood alone, and looked almost as stricken as Maddie. What in the world had happened between those two?

Over the next few minutes, almost everybody in the room came over to tell Madison how much they had admired her father. Personally, I would have been very uncomfortable with all these people seeing me at my most vulnerable, but Maddie seemed to gain consolation from it. She sniffed softly, and wiped at her eyes, her expression sweetly sad as she greeted her friends.

When I cry, which is almost never, I look like I have two black eyes and a big old red clown nose. I know because I cried plenty when my dad left.

Thankfully, the opening event only lasted another hour, and the microsecond it was over, I stuffed Maddie into her car. It was early evening, and we'd gone straight to the reunion event, so we had yet to unload our stuff after the drive down from D.C. I was more than ready to put my feet up and relax.

I drove through the quickly dimming streets, and Maddie, still sniffling sweetly, guided me toward the house where we'd be staying for the duration. Personally, I looked forward to a hot shower and a soft bed. I felt totally, completely, drained.

"So," I asked, in an effort to get Maddie to think of something besides the loss of her father. "What's your mom like?"

Out of the corner of my eye, I saw her shrug. "Just Mom."

"Didn't you say she works for a lawyer?"

"The largest firm in the area, actually. She's been a legal secretary for as long as I can remember."

"Sounds interesting." Actually, it sounded beyond boring, but I couldn't exactly say that.

I steered Madison's cute little red Chevy Aveo around a corner and pulled up the driveway she indicated. The headlights and a porch light illuminated a home that could be the model for gingerbread houses—except for one thing.

"You didn't tell me your mom's house was purple." Purple, mind you. Not violet or lavender or plum. This was bright, unadulterated purple.

There was silence from the other seat, and I looked toward my friend. Madison stared open-mouthed toward the house.

I climbed out of the car, and I saw Madison was doing the same thing on the other side. "It looks really nice," I said.

Madison, who still stared open-mouthed toward the place, didn't answer.

A pink Cadillac pulled in beside us, and a balding middle-aged man in a spandex Spiderman costume minus the mask, climbed out. My camera was in my hand before I thought about it, and I snapped shots of this out-of-the-ordinary person. He aimed a smile in my direction before turning to my open-mouthed friend.

"You must be Madison," he said. "I've heard so much about you," he held out his hand to her. "I'm Henry, your mother's boyfriend."

As I watched Maddie's eyes widen even more, I was suddenly very, very glad I'd come.

I wouldn't have missed this for the world.

The Ugly Truth

Chapter 2

The front door of the purple house opened, and a tall, beautiful woman stepped out onto the porch.

"Margaret," the man in the Spiderman suit said. "Look who's here!"

"Madison! I'm so glad to see you!" The woman in the doorway hurried out to embrace her daughter.

"Hi, Mom. I'm sorry I haven't visited in so long."

Maddie's voice struck such a downcast note; the sound of it made a tiny hole in my heart.

"You've been busy. I understand." Margaret kept an arm around Madison as she turned. "And you must be Stephie. It's so nice to finally meet you."

"Nice to meet you, too." I smiled toward the vibrant woman, whose light brown hair had only a touch of gray. Her bright smile, her khaki pants and crisp sapphire blue blouse all complimented the aura of a woman who seemed far too young to have a daughter a mere year and eight months from thirty. I thought of the workouts and beauty treatments my mother endured in an effort to hold back the signs of passing time. I was sure she'd envy this woman who so naturally radiated youth.

Margaret beckoned to us. "Come on in, the mosquitoes will eat us alive out here."

"It's purple," Madison said, staring hard toward the house.

Margaret chuckled as she wrapped an arm around her daughter, and edged her toward the front porch.

Spiderman held the door as I followed Maddie and her mother inside. They'd moved through the small foyer and turned to go into the living room when Madison suddenly stopped, causing me to bump into her.

*"Mom?"*

The shock and disbelief in her voice had my curiosity bouncing up and down, and I edged around Maddie's body in an effort to see the room.

It was like stepping outdoors on a bright, happy, spring day. The walls were sky blue, and the slipcovers were mint green with bright yellow flowers. The coffee and end tables were rich brown with tiny flowers painted up the legs as if they had grown there.

There were real flowers in pots, sending out a soft, sweet scent throughout the room. The curtain fabric was a colorful mosaic of sunflower yellow, sage green, brilliant indigo, and sunset red. It was gorgeous, and the artist part of me was ecstatic. I raised my camera to capture the sight. "This is great! Did you decorate it yourself?"

"Henry helped me."

"I helped with the grunt work, but the decorating was all her," Henry said, pride obvious in his voice. "Margaret's a very artistic person."

"Well, thank you!" Margaret said, as her face went pink.

The woman was blushing. How cool!

Madison stared at her mother, sort of like she was wondering who this person was. "Mom, could I speak with you for a moment?" Her voice was pitched high enough as to be reminiscent of her earlier squeals.

"I made some iced tea," Margaret said. "You can help me bring it in here." Together they walked into the kitchen, leaving Spidey and me alone in the living room.

"Nice suit," I told him, as we made ourselves at home on the couch.

"Thank you," he said. "The children love it."

Huh? "Children?"

"I volunteer at the children's hospital a couple of days a week. I just came from there."

"That's so great!" There was clearly more to this man than met the eye, and I immediately wanted to get to know him better. "I couldn't deal with sick kids," I told him. "I volunteer at a homeless shelter, and we get children in there way too often. Breaks my heart."

"Breaks mine too, but I love the feeling that maybe I can bring some happiness into the little darlings' lives."

"You're a good man...Henry, right?"

He held out a hand to her. "Henry Thomas at your service."

"Like the kid in *E.T.*?"

He chuckled. "You know, I've never seen that movie."

"You should, it's really great." I shook his hand. "And my name is Stephie."

"Stephie what?"

"My last name's Stephanova. Stephie's a nickname."

"So what's your first name?"

Oh good grief, you can't slide anything past these people. "I prefer to just go with Stephie, if you don't mind."

He inclined his head as he gave me a soft smile. "Whatever the lady wants."

A real gentleman? I thought they were creatures of legend. Like Bigfoot. I gave him my very best smile. "Thank you, kind sir."

I studied his warm eyes for a moment, but quickly became uncomfortable and looked away. When I did, I caught a glimpse of a picture above the fireplace, and crossed the room for a better look. The painting was clear, colorful, and almost impressionistic with its soft edges and exaggeration of features. "This is great!"

"Margaret's a talented artist."

*Margaret.* I leaned closer, and sure enough, the signature read, "Margaret Clark."

Henry came to stand beside me. "I'm very proud of her."

"You should be. This is amazing."

The sound of footsteps announced the return of Madison and her mother, who carried trays with iced tea and snacks. Maddie looked a bit teary-eyed, but Margaret was smiling.

"This painting is wonderful, Mrs. Clark," I said. "You're very talented!"

"Thank you, and please call me Margaret."

"You're painting again, Mom?" Madison's voice sounded like she'd been sucking on a helium-filled balloon.

"I started again about a year ago," Mrs. Clark…Margaret…said.

"I encouraged her," Henry said. "Talent like hers shouldn't go to waste."

Madison's gaze swung to Henry, and I could see

distrust and barely restrained hostility flash in her eyes.

"Henry volunteers at the children's hospital," I told her. "That's why the costume."

Madison didn't say a word, she just stared at him.

Henry gave a small, sad sigh. "The only bad thing about my volunteer work is it takes time from my business. I need to get going."

He gave Margaret a quick kiss on her lips, then nodded toward Madison and me. "Glad to meet you."

"Glad to meet you too," I told him, and I meant it.

Madison muttered, "Me too," as Henry left.

Margaret closed and locked the front door, then turned back to us. "I know you don't like me seeing him, Maddie, but Henry has been very good for me."

Madison spun and glared at her mother. "How can you betray Daddy like this?"

"I loved your father very much, but he's been gone *ten years*."

"I don't care how long it's been, he'll always be my father." Madison spun and tore up the stairs like a banshee was right on her heels.

The sigh that blew from Margaret seemed to push out all her stuffing. Her head drooped forward and her eyes closed.

I decided to venture a try. "This festival thing is hard on her."

"I know," Margaret whispered. "And I know this isn't the best time to spring something like her mother's boyfriend on her, but that isn't really something you can talk about over the phone or in a letter." She looked at me then. "We'd thought Henry would be gone before you two got here, but he got held up at the hospital so he didn't get here until you were already here and..."

She shrugged. "Well, we'd decided we weren't going to hide our relationship from Maddie. It wouldn't be fair to either of them."

"Henry seems like a very nice man."

A smile pulled at the corners of her mouth. "He's a sweetheart."

She motioned toward the couch, and we sat. "Virgil died and Maddie left for college soon after. I felt like I'd lost all direction in my life. I'd been wife and mother for so long I'd forgotten who I was. For a long time I just floated aimlessly through my life. Then I got to know Henry, and he encouraged me to think outside the box. For a long time we were just friends." She shrugged. "Then one night we kissed, and it was magic."

"That sounds wonderful."

She looked at me then, almost as if she'd forgotten I was there. "I'm sorry. I'm sure you aren't interested in an old woman's rambling."

"You are *so* not old."

"To someone your age I am."

"No, you aren't, and thank you for sharing your story." I looked down at my hands for a moment. "I just hope one day I'll find a man I'm willing to put up with for the rest of my life." Yikes! Why did I just say that?

Margaret patted my shoulder. "You will. You just have to keep your eyes open and don't settle for less than the very best."

I smiled at the bright confidence in her eyes. "Thank you."

"You're very welcome." She stood. "Now I'm going to get some dinner on the table. I hope you like chicken."

24

"I love chicken. What can I do to help?"

"Honestly, if you'd make sure Maddie's all right it would be much appreciated."

"Okay, but if I'm not back by the time dinner's ready you have to promise to send in the troops."

She chuckled. "Will do."

I turned and hurried up the stairs. I peeked in the first room I passed. Obviously Margaret's bedroom, with the beautiful classic furniture and the wide range of muted color.

There was a bathroom, and the next door was closed. Beyond was one more room, and I could see the edges of canvasses from where I stood. That must be Margaret's art studio. I itched to go in there, but my responsibility was to my friend. So I gently knocked on the closed door, then opened it without waiting for an invitation.

Maddie was sprawled across one of the white twin beds covered with matching pink and violet bedspreads.

"Are you okay?" I asked.

She chewed her lower lip for a moment before she answered. "I'm sure you think I should just accept my mother has a...." I saw her swallow. "A friend. It's not that easy, though. Not for me."

"I understand."

"No, you don't. Not really."

I sat beside her. "You're right. I have no idea what you're feeling. You had a *Leave It to Beaver* childhood. It has to be really hard to let that perfection go."

Madison allowed me a rueful smile. "My family isn't perfect, long way from it. Witness today, for instance."

I snorted. "Hey, if that's all you got, I hope you

never meet *my* family."

Maddie touched my arm. "I know your life was hard. I'm sorry."

"It was hard for you to lose your dad." I shrugged. "Besides, I've put all that family crap behind me."

"No, you haven't."

I opened my mouth to tell her what I thought of her, but when I looked into her eyes, I changed my mind. I was sure she was wrong, I was well beyond that ugly time in my life, but it seemed mean to argue with a woman who'd been through so much grief.

She pulled herself up and propped against the headboard. "I guess I can't imagine anybody with Mom except Dad."

I nodded in support, but my mind whipped through the mental family album, the one where my own mother married within six months after my father left. She'd pushed through the divorce—it's amazing what money can do—and sent me and my brother straight into hell.

"Did Mom send you up here to talk to me?"

"To check on you, not to use my devious charm to make you see her side."

Maddie picked at the girly pink and violet bedspread. "I guess I should go and talk to her."

"I think you should."

She grabbed me in a big hug, all but knocking me off the bed in the process. "You're a good friend, Buffy."

She got away before I could pinch her. Nobody calls me that. Nobody. I refuse to have a name that's half bitchy-richy and half run-around-slaying-things-person. Stupid TV show.

To give Maddie and her mom a few minutes alone,

I lay across the bed and surveyed the room where my friend had grown up. It was girly, of course. Not that I'm not feminine, mind you, I just have a more Bohemian taste. Maddie is all about frills and pastels.

The walls were a soft cerulean, the furniture white with gold trim. Everything else was a mixture of pink, blue, violet and white. The pictures on the wall were of kittens and ballerinas, with a poster of Johnny Depp in full pirate costume thrown in to keep the place from seeming too little-girly.

For one, awful moment, I was a bit jealous. No, I did not wish I had a frilly, girly room back home. Wouldn't fit me, or that cold mansion I grew up in. What had my heart longing, I guess, was the idea of a comfortable home, a bedroom decorated to suit my taste, a mother and a father who loved me.

Mom had wasted no time getting rid of a gorgeous red and gold rug I'd snagged at a thrift store, put a decorative fringe on the edge, and used as a bedspread. I'd loved the effect, but she couldn't get past the "it's a *rug*!" idea.

Okay, this was ridiculous. To distract myself, I took a visual inventory. Dolls, stuffed animals, trophies, silver comb and brush set. Wait a minute. Trophies? Interesting.

I pulled myself off the bed and went over to the white shelves on the wall over the desk. As I got closer, my heart began to pound, and it seemed to be hard to push and pull the air in and out of my lungs. Little metal cheerleaders waved pompoms on top of the trophies. Cheerleader? Oh no. Say it ain't so!

Sadly, the truth was right in front of me. There were trophies, awards, and pictures; group and team.

And in the team picture, not only did Maddie's too-perfect face look out at me, Liza was also among the short-skirted crowd. No wonder they squealed so much. Sigh.

As I stared at the shrine to popular kids, I wondered if I was going to be able to handle this new information. Madison Clark, my nearest and dearest friend, had not only been a high school cheerleader, she'd been *head* cheerleader.

I took a couple of steps backward and all but fell onto the end of one of the beds. I propped my elbows on my knees and let my suddenly too-heavy head drop onto my hands. I'd worked with her; I'd shared an apartment with her; I'd trusted her with the truth about my background.

And now this.

I couldn't take it. I had to get out of the room. I scurried out into the hall and took a long breath of non-cheerleader air.

I didn't hear any yelling from downstairs, so that was a good sign. Probably.

I'd head down there, but I'd take my time about it, give Cheerleader Girl a bit of space, and myself a little time to adapt.

Of course, that presented a whole different problem. Just how long could I dawdle between here and the kitchen. I could snoop, and I have to admit, I do love to snoop. It didn't seem right though, snooping in my best friend's house. On the other hand, she was a cheerleader, for goodness sake. What other dark, disturbing secrets was she hiding?

I headed straight for the room I'd wanted to explore ever since I'd caught a glimpse of it.

In my defense, the door was open.

Brushes, paints, and other supplies were neatly stored. An easel held a painting of a man who looked familiar from the photo of him Maddie had on her dresser. It was Virgil Clark, Maddie's dad.

I had never met Maddie's father, when I looked at that painting I felt I knew him. As if Mrs. Clark had somehow captured the essence of her late husband on the canvas. It was an amazing thing to see. The woman was incredibly talented.

I saw a variety of landscapes around the room. Apparently she rarely did portraits. And that was a serious shame.

The ding of a doorbell brought my attention back to the present, and I headed for the door. I hadn't quite made it when I caught a glimpse of a painting that seemed to be of some sort of furry creature. I hadn't seen anything other than landscapes and one portrait, so I took a moment to move the blank canvas blocking my view. And stepped back in shock.

The painting was a portrait after all—of a Bigfoot. Sharp and detailed, the piece seemed to capture a personality just as much as the one on the easel. Why had she painted a mythical creature? A creature that seemed alive. A creature with a soul. Maybe she was that imaginative.

Or maybe she'd simply painted what she saw.

Chapter 3

The sound of voices reminded me I was in someone else's house, snooping around where I wasn't invited. I pulled the blank canvas back in front of Mr. Sasquatch and headed for the stairs.

"Stephie," Mrs. Clark called from the bottom. "I'd like you to meet Aunt Octavia."

Her auntie was not even five feet tall and wore jeans, white sneakers, a bright orange sweater, and carried a black purse about half the size she was. Her hair was mostly black, blended with gray. She was probably around seventy or so, and she was about the cutest little thing I'd ever seen.

"It's very nice to meet you," I said, as I reached toward her. Instead of shaking my hand, though, she turned it over and leaned close to scrutinize my palm.

"Your lifeline splits. A major life decision is coming."

Yeah, okay. "Well, thank you for your insight."

"Aunt Octavia!"

Cutie turned. "Madison!"

Then they hugged and I smiled. Maddie was five-seven, and the adorable palm reader didn't even make her shoulder.

"I'm so glad to see you, Aunt Octavia," Maddie said.

"My sweet Madison. Always with an aura of

success."

Great, I get decisions and Maddie gets success. But then, Psychic Lady was *her* relative. At least she hadn't done the stereotypical tall, dark, handsome stranger line—and just why did those words make my thoughts go straight to Jake Blackwood?

"We'd love to have you stay for dinner." Mrs. Clark said.

"Oh no, dear," Octavia said. "I have several errands to run before dark. I just wanted to stop by and see my sweet Madison." She took my hand again and held it. "And meet this Stephie I've been hearing about."

I tried to extricate my hand, but she held on. Her eyes dropped closed, and she swayed a little. I was beginning to wonder if she was having a stroke or something, but then her eyes popped open.

"Beware a rabbit the color of grass."

She let go of my hand then, so I stepped back. "Thanks, I'll be sure to do that."

Auntie Cute but Weird turned and strolled out the door.

"She is such a sweet woman." Maddie had a big smile on her face.

I didn't want to admit what I thought about that "sweet woman," so I kept my big mouth shut.

"Let's eat," Mrs. Clark said, and headed toward the kitchen with Maddie close behind.

Three hours later Maddie and I were in her childhood bedroom, sprawled on the twin beds, leaned against our respective headboards while our bodies digested a large and excellent baked chicken dinner with sides of sweet carrots, corn, and to-die-for mashed potatoes.

"You and your mother seem to have resolved your conflict," I said. Dinner conversation had been a little on the strained side, but nobody had tried to kill anybody. In my family that would have counted for a wonderful night. Hell, in my family it would be a miracle.

Maddie leaned against her headboard and closed her eyes, an expression of pain and longing coloring her perfect features. "I love her, and part of me realizes Daddy's been gone ten years, but part of me wants to scream at the thought of her with another man. She said Dad was her soul mate, how can she betray him like this?"

I wanted to go to her, to sit beside her and support her, but Maddie didn't always respond well to touchy-feely and I was afraid my nearness would only irritate her more. I wanted to remind her she'd said herself it had been ten years. I knew she was being unrealistic and wildly unfair to her mom. But I knew exactly how she felt. My dad hadn't died a hero. In fact, he'd just up and left us. But when Mom hooked up with my stepdad, I felt like she was betraying Daddy. Yeah, I know, crazy. But the brain and the heart don't always see eye to eye. And did Mom really have to marry a jackass?

I shook away the contemplation of things I couldn't have done anything about even when they were happening. I figured the only thing I could really do for my friend was to lighten up the conversation, or at least get it going in another direction. Besides, my curiosity was jumping up and down trying to get my attention. "I didn't know you believed in psychics."

Madison shrugged without opening her eyes.

"Mostly I don't. Psychics are generally scam artists or fakes. Aunt Octavia, though, she's different. She has a gift."

"So I'm going to be ravaged by a wild green bunny?"

Maddie shrugged. "The spirits don't always give her straightforward information."

"Therefore, open to interpretation."

Her eyes opened then, the bright blue popping. "No. What she says may sound strange, but it will make sense. And soon. Be careful, okay?"

I glared. "So says you, with your 'aura of success'."

Maddie closed her eyes again, as a cat-that-ate-the-canary smile pulled at her lips. "I can't help it because the spirits like me."

I groaned. "I get life decisions and you get *The New York Times*."

"For all you know, your choice might be between *The New York Times* and *National Geographic*."

"Or *The National Enquirer*."

"I hear they pay well."

"Bite me." Out of the corner of my eye, I saw the shelf of trophies. "You were even successful in cheerleading, huh?"

Her eyes popped open again, and this time I could see worry in the depths. Did I say how smart my friend is?

"Oh crap, I forgot to have Mom hide that stuff."

"Ashamed of your short-skirted exploits?"

She gave me the evil eye. "No. I just knew how you'd react."

I flopped back, my hand over my eyes in overacted

distress. "How could you not tell me?"

"I wasn't sure you'd ever forgive me."

Through narrowed eyes I was pretty sure I saw her lips twitch. She'd better not smile. "You might be right."

"I know it was stupid, but I was young."

"I can't believe my best friend is one of *them*."

"Them?"

"The enemy." I swallowed hard. "You were one of the...gag... *popular* kids."

The snort had my gaze jerking toward her. She wouldn't dare. I looked at Maddie, and she lost it. My mean cheerleader-type-friend laughed so hard the bed shook. Dang it!

"I'm going to kill you later," I told her, "when you aren't expecting it. Slowly and painfully."

That just had her laughing harder.

I sat back and tried to ignore my traitorous friend. Cheerleader, popular, gorgeous. And she thinks I'm funny. Ugh. Maybe murder wasn't good enough. Maybe I should cancel her subscription to *Vogue*.

She finally got herself calmed down and wiped at her eyes. "I'm sorry."

"Whatever."

The next thing I knew she was stretched out on the bed beside me, propped on an elbow, her chin supported by a hand. "Do you think you can ever forgive me?"

It's her eyes. Being mad at those big blue eyes is kinda like smacking a puppy upside the head. I can't do it. So I guess I'll have to forgive her. Eventually.

"Well?" she asked.

"Maybe. Someday," I conceded.

"Thank you." She gave me a quick squeeze, kissed the top of my head, then jumped up and rushed for the door. "Dibs on the bathroom."

The rat.

I lay back and glared at the photos on the top of her dresser. It's amazing how even people you think you know can surprise you.

While I waited for her to finish her beauty routine—which, in spite of her natural envy-producing gorgeousness—could take a while, I decided to download the pictures I took last night to my computer.

I booted up my laptop and looked through the myriad shots. One in particular caught my attention, the one of Steve looking at Liza. For the second time in just a few hours, I felt a touch of jealousy. I'd give a lot to have a man look at me like that. But I knew it was highly unlikely. Things like that just don't happen to women like me. I had way too much baggage. Any good man would run in the opposite direction.

I shoved the sadness from my head and pulled up a game of spider solitaire. Maybe boredom would dull the sudden, odd loneliness.

****

That night, I lay in the dark room for hours, listening to the crickets and cicadas outside. Damn. The sounds reminded me of Alabama, of my childhood home, of the hell I swore I'd never return to.

I rolled over. Again. And tried to relax, but the strange house, the long trip, and finding out my closest friend had been a cheerleader was more than my brain could handle.

I slipped out of the room and tiptoed down the stairs. I'd seen the screened-in back porch through a window during dinner and complimented Mrs. Clark on it. She said her property backed onto the woods and they'd built the porch to take advantage of the view. After we ate she took me out there, and I'd fallen in love. Outside, but safe from the flies and mosquitoes that are the bane of Southern life, the porch with simple wicker chairs and a small wicker table was a place for quiet contemplation. A place that felt safe.

That's where I went now. The full moon cast its bright glow onto the woods, and bits of the light overflowed to illuminate the porch. I leaned back and luxuriated in the soft light and the quiet, fresh air.

I might not miss my mom's whining, or the yelling, or my stepdad's quick backhand. But sometimes I missed the country. Sometimes the thick air, the masses of people, and the rush of big city life made me want to go running.

Movement near a tree caught my attention and I narrowed my eyes to get a better look. Whatever was out there, it was pretty big. Large dog? Maybe a retriever, a German Shepherd, or even a Great Dane.

Then I saw something that looked suspiciously like an arm. Yikes. Bear, maybe?

I slowly got to my feet and backed toward the door. The last thing I wanted was a confrontation with a grizzly. And the screen door would be about as effective as a broken fly swat in repelling an attack.

The animal moved a little, and I could see it was roughly the shape of a man, but furry, very furry. Yep, bear. Had to be. I backed faster.

Just as I opened the kitchen door, the animal turned and looked right at me, then spun and headed rapidly in the other direction.

On two feet.

Bears run on all fours.

That thing looked like...well, like a Bigfoot.

I turned and got inside the house as fast as I could, locking the door tight behind me. Obviously I was waaay too tired. That's all it could be, right?

Chapter 4

"Wake up, sleepyhead."

I opened my eyes and cringed at the bright light coming from the window. "Since when are you a morning person?"

Maddie grinned. "Since shopping is involved."

It figured. Shopping, the Holy Grail of the slim and stylish. "Fine, I'll catch up with you later." I pulled the covers over my head.

Two seconds later, my covers were all the way at the foot of the bed. "No way José. Liza will be here in a half hour, and you're going to the mall with us."

I groaned. Maybe if I ignored her she'd go away. Or I could bargain with her, or bribe her...

Or I could get my ass up before she thought of something really mean to do to me. Madison Clark may look like a sweet person, but I've seen her dark side, and she scares me. So I did what any red-blooded, relatively sane person would do: I went shopping.

****

An hour later, Madison, Liza and I were at the Ugly Creek Mall. Yep, that's right, there's a mall with that ridiculous name. Just to throw another curve into the game, the mall was about ten miles northeast of Ugly Creek. It was big, relatively new, and very nice. When I commented on the situation, Maddie told me Ugly Creek is near enough to Knoxville that the mall draws shoppers from there. Personally, I think it's tourists looking for a Bigfoot that's powering the shopping dollar. We parked on the north side, near J.C. Penney's, then we power-walked into the land of retail.

Madison Clark is an excellent reporter. She charms information out of even the most reluctant source, and she has seemingly never-ending energy when she's going after a story. All that pales, though, in the wake of her ability to shop until everybody else drops. Except for Liza, who kept up without even breaking a sweat. Must be the fresh air, 'cause they grow 'em tough here.

After six stores and three trips back to the car to stash bags, we stopped long enough to grab lunch at the food court. I would have loved to just sit, relax, and people watch. My companions, however, were soon chomping at the bit. I tried hard to delay them, but nothing stands between ex-cheerleaders and retailers primed to take their money. It was barely twenty minutes before we headed back to the stores.

As we rushed headlong toward a high-end clothing store, I caught a glimpse of an odd little man. He had to be less than four feet tall and wore all green, which contrasted sharply with his bright red beard. It was all I could do not to point and shout, "Leprechaun!" But that was impossible. Right?

I realized I'd stopped dead in place when I heard some seriously bad language emanating from more than one person behind me. That realization brought me out of my daze and I shook my head to clear it. When I looked back, the man had vanished. "Losing my mind," I muttered, and rushed off to find the Shopping Twins before they forgot I was with them and left me at the mercy of tourists and leprechauns.

A couple of hours later I was dawdling in a stall in the ladies room at Sears, not so much because I needed to go as because I needed to rest. While I was hiding—I mean making use of the facilities—I eavesdropped on a couple of women. I told you, I love to people-watch...and people-listen.

"Hey, Ethel what are you wearing to the big shindig?" a woman's voice said.

"I got a new pantsuit," a second voice said. "It's blue and white, and so comfortable. I can't wait to wear it to the party."

"Sounds good. I just thought I'd wear that green dress of mine."

"Goodness, Crystal, is Frank so stingy he won't let you get something for the big event of the year?"

"No. I just didn't want to spend the money. You know, with the economy being so bad and everything."

"Well, you have to get something new. Come on and we'll find you a nice outfit."

I peeked out at this point, through a tiny crack between the door and frame. Just as I thought, a couple of middle-aged women. And while it was pretty cool to hear two older women discussing fashion, I was about to open the door when something about the tone and the way the woman dropped the volume on the next words stopped me in mid lock-flip.

"All right," Crystal said. "I am looking forward to the party. I heard Abukcheech's giving Nootau headaches."

"I heard that too. I tell you what, it's hard enough to raise a human kid, and Abukcheech is almost as tall as most grown men. I don't know how the Dyami do it."

Then one of the women lowered her voice to the point I could just barely hear. "Those Yankee tourists would be fit to be tied if they knew about the party."

"You got that right."

They were laughing as they went out the door.

I waited quietly until I was sure they were gone before I came out of the stall. Interesting. Very interesting.

I was headed out to hunt down my co-shoppers, when I heard my name and turned to see Jake Blackwood's grinning face. In spite of my half-hearted attempt to hold it back, I felt a big smile pull at my lips. And my feet seemed to think I needed to be closer to tall, sexy, and trouble.

"You're out shopping, huh?" he asked.

I shrugged. "Mostly Maddie and Liza are shopping. I just got dragged along."

"A woman who doesn't like shopping? Wow."

"I didn't say I don't like to shop. I just don't much like malls."

"Really?"

"Yeah, I'm more of a thrift store gal."

"Why am I not surprised?"

The warmth in his eyes sent a thrill up and down my body. Yum, he was one handsome man. Too bad there was that whole conflict thing with my closest friend.

"I'd better be going," my mouth said. My feet edged a little closer to Jake.

"I own an antique shop downtown," he said. "Maybe you could come by before you go back to D.C."

"I'd like that." Was I grinning like a teenager? Did

I care?

His hand touched mine. It was a gentle, brief touch, but it sent hot tingles up my arm. "See you around." He turned and walked away, leaving me gasping for breath.

As I headed for the meeting place with Liza and Maddie, I could still feel exactly where Jake's fingers had connected with mine. It was almost like he'd branded me somehow with his touch.

"There you are, slow poke." Hands on hips, Madison glared. "I was beginning to think you'd gone home without us."

I wish. Except for running into Jake, and that odd conversation, today had mostly just been exhausting. "No, I'm still here."

Maddie wrapped an arm around me. "Will you relax and enjoy yourself. This is supposed to be a fun day."

"I'm just not into shopping the same way you are."

Maddie sighed and looked toward Liza. "Stephie isn't into fashion, at least not fashion from this century."

"Bite me."

"You have to admit, malls are magical places." Her face lit with excitement. "How can you not breathe in the sweet smell of this place and not want to spend money?"

Subliminal messages? Brainwashing at cheerleader camp? Or maybe I just didn't get the shopping gene.

"There's a sale at Marshall's," Liza said.

"Let's go." Maddie grabbed my arm and we took off.

For a while it was same old, same old. But then something delicate and blue caught my attention. It turned out to be the most gorgeous blouse I'd ever seen. Soft and lacy, it was feminine and sexy in a restrained sort of way. I took it off the rack with trembling fingers. My size. And on sale.

"You have to try that on."

I smiled toward my friend. "Okay."

"And you need pants or a skirt to go with it."

I tried to groan quietly, so she wouldn't hear.

"And shoes," Liza put in.

"And a purse." The excitement in Maddie's voice apparently was contagious, because soon I was caught up in it. I actually found not one outfit, but three. Plus gray slacks I could pair with a suit I had at home. All on sale, and all excellent buys. Or at least that's how I rationalized my purchases. Besides, I was on vacation. Right? I deserved to live it up a bit.

We finally headed toward the car. Liza and Madison, being much more accustomed to schlepping armloads of shopping bags, were way ahead of me. The bright sun of the parking lot slowed me down, and I stumbled a bit going from the sidewalk to the asphalt. By this time, sunglasses firmly in place, the Shopping Sisters were almost to Liza's car. I sighed and started after them.

The car came from nowhere, or at least that's the way it seemed. It rushed straight at me, and at first I felt frozen, the way it sometimes happens in dreams. The green metal vehicle bore down at me, and I stood there like an idiot. Surely it would stop.

Green. The color of grass. *Beware!*

My brain kicked into gear, and I dove for the sidewalk.

I looked up just in time to see a VW emblem on the

back of the squat, boxy vehicle as it skidded out of the parking lot. At the last second, I caught the name on the back of the seriously ugly car, and suddenly wanted to sit on the sidewalk and laugh my guts out. Rabbit. The dang car was an old Volkswagen Rabbit.

"Are you all right?" Maddie yelled, as she and Liza ran toward me.

"Green," I muttered, as I pulled myself up off the sidewalk. "VW. Green. Rabbit."

"You hit your head, didn't you?" We'll get you to the hospital. You probably have a concussion."

"I'm okay," I told Maddie. "Thanks to your Aunt Octavia."

Understanding crossed her face. "The warning."

I nodded. "Beware a rabbit the color of grass."

"Wow!"

"What the heck are you two talking about?"

"I'll tell you on the way home," Maddie told Liza.

They helped me gather my bags and we walked— very carefully—across the lot to Liza's silver Nova.

Due to the excitement, we all decided a snack was in order, so we stopped by a small ice cream shop. I was ignoring the stinging of my knees in order to savor a butterscotch sundae with nuts, when Liza said, "What are you two wearing tonight?"

"What's tonight?" I asked, hoping the disappointment didn't show in my voice. I'd sort of hoped for a quiet evening and an early bedtime.

"Talent night," Maddie said.

Oh great. "What kind of talent?"

Madison's crisp, light laugh washed over me. "Relax, Steph. It's really very nice. There's a dance school and a singer I can't vouch for, but the highlight of the evening is a band called Women of the Hills. They're Celtic, all women, and very, very good. You'll enjoy yourself. Honest."

I wasn't sure I believed her. Plus, I was still exhausted and in pain—but not so much I didn't enjoy my sundae.

****

I could smell rain in the early evening air. Even though the moisture in the atmosphere made the heat more oppressive, I relished the fresh aroma. Sure I'd smelled rain in D.C., but it was different in this more rural area. Instead of vehicle exhaust, the aroma of growing plants spiced the scent. I felt warm nostalgia wash over me as I thought of cool water spewing from a green water hose on a hot summer day.

I hoped it would be a while before the rain started though, for the sake of the festival in progress on the Ugly Creek Courthouse square. Yes it's true. I'd be perfectly happy if the whole thing got washed away, but the people in town really seemed to be looking forward to the show. Who am I to wish rain on their parade...I mean talent show.

I settled into a green and white lawn chair near Madison (orange and white), Mrs. Clark (blue and white), Liz, and Steve (green and white, blue and white, respectively). The dance recital currently playing out on the raised wooden stage in front of us was a sweet reminder of how some things never change. At the moment, a half dozen little girls in black and yellow leotards, black tights, black tap shoes, white wings and headbands with bumblebee antennae attached were step-ball-changing to Frank Sinatra's "Ain't She Sweet."

"They're so cute!" Madison said.

"Especially the little one," Liza said.

They really were cute. They were probably five or six years old, except the adorable blonde on the end, who couldn't be more than four. Someday, I found myself thinking. It wasn't something I allowed myself to contemplate very often, this illogical yearning to be a wife and mother. My childhood was enough to make me leery of the very idea. But the sight of those beautiful little kids had odd desires rising to the surface. Even odder, I found myself wondering what a child with Jake would look like.

Shaking myself out of the odd and unwanted train of thought, I focused on the program in front of me. The dance recital was over, and the singer took the stage.

She was probably mid-teens, thin, gorgeous, the daughter of one of the big-shots on the town council. Nobody in our little group had any expectation she could actually sing. And from the rumblings around me, nobody else seemed to think so either.

She looked composed and confident, but I caught the trembling of her hand as she took the microphone. She was nervous. Suddenly I felt for the poor thing. Likely this was a bigger, scarier version of "stand the kid in the living room and make her perform for our friends."

Then she began to sing.

The entire crowd went silent. I heard Maddie gasp beside me.

"She's wonderful!" Liza said.

I felt the smile pull at my face. The girl was absolutely amazing. Her voice was clear and pure; her range seemed to be endless. There was something magical about her I couldn't begin to describe.

She was only slated to sing one song, but the audience clamored until she performed four songs, and only ended there because she sang from recorded music and that was all she'd brought with her.

The applause continued even while the upcoming band began their setup. I wondered how it would feel to follow up that kid. What was her name? I had several clear shots of her and would love it if I could give her a print or two. And maybe get her autograph. That girl was going to be a star one day.

If small town life didn't spoil her dreams.

Letting it go for now, I turned back to the upcoming performance.

As Maddie had said, the band was Celtic, and I was a little unsure about that. What did I know about Celtic music? Nothing, that's what. I had no idea what I was in for, but they ganged up on me and insisted I'd enjoy myself.

Strangely enough, I did.

Women of the Hills was a wonderful band made up of interesting and talented women, and just watching them was a treat.

The long, thin whistles were different sizes and colors, and the whistler coaxed amazing sounds from her instruments. The drummer held her drum with one hand, and flipped the other back and forth hitting the instrument with both ends of a small stick so rapidly the movement was a blur. As I watched with awe, I wondered if she wouldn't have a sore wrist in the morning. I would, that's for sure—not that I could have done what she did even if somebody held a gun to my head.

There were also two guitarists, one of whom played banjo for a couple of pieces, and a fiddler. They all sang at one time or another, even the whistler. The music the band played was fun and relaxing. Healing, Mrs. Clark said. I could believe it. A deep, painful rip in my soul, one that I didn't even know was there, began to close in response to the sweet sounds coming from the temporary stage.

A glance toward Madison told me my friend wasn't so relaxed. Her shoulders were too high and close to her ears, and her posture was tense. Most telling were the covert glances Maddie pretended she wasn't shooting over her shoulder.

Even before I looked, I knew Jake was there.

He sat at the very edge of the crowd, tapping his foot to the rhythm of the music. As I watched, his gaze slowly slid to meet mine. He smiled, and I thought my heart was going to jump right out of my chest and race over to him. But then he turned back to watching the performers.

An almost overwhelming urge to go back and sit with him danced inside me. He was alone, and the people around me all had strong ties to each other. They probably wouldn't even notice my absence.

Then I looked toward Madison, and the expression of pain pulling at my friend's face tore away any thoughts of leaving her. It wouldn't be right. I still had no idea why Maddie and Jake seemed to care about and hate each other simultaneously, but I wasn't about to be disloyal to a friend just because I had the hots for a guy. How low would that be?

As low as a mother choosing a man over her

children?

Shaking my head, I fought to clear away memories of my mother. I wasn't her. I was nothing like her.

I squeezed Madison's arm, and she smiled weakly toward me. I sighed, leaned back, and tried to focus on the show. It was nice here, sitting in a lawn chair on the grass and listening to music while the evening breeze rustled the leaves and relieved the damp heat of the day. Wistful sadness deep inside my heart confused me, until I realized to my surprise I was homesick. It had been a very long time since I'd even thought about Alabama, much less missed the place. Yeah, I thought about my little brother a lot, mostly with self-reproach. But think about the place where I grew up? Never.

I was now, though. Surrounded by the trees, the fresh air, music in the park. I found myself smiling at the memories—and wondering if I was losing my mind.

Before I could sink too deeply into the mire of mental distress, a deep, jarring sound pulled me back into the present. I glanced toward the band, but they were between numbers. Actually, the band members frowned and glanced around as if they too were confused about the source of the low-pitched rumble.

The crowd was muttering. I scanned the area, but saw nothing that could explain the odd noise. I'd lived in D.C. long enough that the thought of terrorists shot into my brain without hesitation. One glance at Maddie told me she was thinking the same thing. She opened her mouth, and I knew she was about to suggest we get the hell away from the current ground zero.

"UFO!"

I jerked around to look toward the kid who'd yelled. Of course my mind went to the obvious:

missiles, bombs on airplanes, bio weapons dropped from the sky.

Then I looked up.

It was mostly a circular, and very bright, orange light, but behind the glow I could see the outline of what looked like a flattened beach ball. It was hard to see specifics, though; I kept having to look away. It was rather like trying to look at the sun, look a little too long and your eyes felt like they'd explode.

My camera was in my hand without conscious thought. I clicked away for a moment, then exchanged the digital for my trusty thirty-five millimeter single lens reflex. Not only might the film catch something the pixels didn't, there would be a negative for proof. I even had enough time to fit a filter over the lens before the light/object zipped away toward the distant mountains. As I watched, whatever had visited the festival disappeared up and over the top of the highest peak.

"Holy crap," Maddie muttered.

I nodded. My sentiments exactly.

Only slowly did I realize the high pitched sound was gone, replaced by an almost unearthly quiet. Little by little the murmur of voices began to grow louder. I looked at Maddie, and she looked at me, wide-eyed and just a bit pale. She turned to speak to her mother and I found myself looking back over my shoulder. Jake looked right at me.

His gaze met mine, and he mouthed, "Whoa."

I nodded, and he smiled. My heart leaped, and other parts of my body warmed and softened. The man was just too freaking good looking for my own good.

Then he looked away, and I turned back to the

front. Music was again filling the air, and I leaned back and tried to relax. I noticed, though, I wasn't the only one who kept glancing upward. Apparently, a UFO wasn't usual even in Ugly Creek.

Thank goodness.

Chapter 5

"Why don't you come with me? It'll be fun, I promise."

"To a cheerleader brunch? Are you serious?"

Madison sighed. "Are you going to hold this cheerleader thing against me for the rest of my life?"

"Of course. What kind of friend do you think I am?" I shoved a bite of bagel into my mouth, and ignored the cute doggie eyes and the sweet pouty lip she was giving me.

"Well fine, if you want to walk around town in nine thousand degree heat, it's not my concern."

I shrugged. "The stores have air conditioning."

She narrowed her perfectly lined, shadowed and mascaraed eyes. "You're going shopping without me. That's the plan. You rat."

I shrugged. "This way, I don't have to sit through a cheerleader brunch, and you don't have to slug through thrift stores and flea markets."

She leaned her head to one side and chewed a shiny coral lip in thought. "Okay. I give. I'll meet you at The Café for lunch."

"Lunch? Aren't you going to a brunch?"

"Yeah, so?"

"Isn't brunch supposed to take the place of both breakfast and lunch?"

She rolled her eyes. "It's a bunch of ex-cheerleaders. They'll be nothing on that table but celery, grapes, and bottled water."

Ah, so Maddie's astonishing metabolism strikes again. "Fine with me. Which café?"

"*The* Café, that's the name."

"Why am I not surprised?"

Maddie chuckled. "Because you're from Crooked Tree Hollow."

I shuddered. "Please don't say that name. Rumor has it if you say it three times, you'll be whisked away to Main Street, in front of the county courthouse."

A gentle hand touched my arm. "Steph, I know you don't like to talk about your past, but if you hold all that pain and anger inside it's just going to fester."

I glared at her. "What do you know about it? You with your perfect cheerleader life."

She didn't even blink. "I know you're in a lot of pain, and I wish you'd let somebody in. You can't handle everything by yourself, Stephanova, no matter what you think."

She turned toward the counter and poured herself a second cup of coffee.

Did she really have to bring up my hometown? Did she have to remind me of all those awful memories, of the hell I'd grown up in? I wanted to lash out at her, to scream, to tell her she had no business telling me I needed to talk about things I seriously just wanted to forget?

Except I'd said similar to her. And I was afraid, very afraid, she might just be right. I really needed to change the subject.

"So, your mom must get up at the crack of dawn." Though we'd crawled out of bed fairly early, she'd already left for work.

Maddie nodded. "She's very devoted to her job. She's been the secretary for Mantuck, Conner, and Holmes for so long they couldn't get by without her. The lawyers think they're in charge, but she's the one who actually runs the place."

I smiled with vicarious pride, but that didn't stop a trickle of envy from moving down my spine. What would it be like to be proud of a mother you loved, who loved and protected you? I swallowed back the pain. I was truly happy for Maddie. And Lord knows she'd had her share of pain. "Your mom seems like a really special person."

"She is." Maddie shoved in the last bite of her bagel and sucked down the rest of her coffee. "Ready?"

I drained my cup. "Let's go."

Twenty minutes later Madison was on her way to a cheerleader function and I was stranded in the middle of a small Southern town armed with nothing more than my purse, two cameras, and a major case of curiosity. Taking a long breath of the fresh, fume-free air, I looked around.

It was like taking a long jump back in time. A narrow street with sidewalks on either side separated opposing walls of one and two story buildings. Some were red brick, some wooden exteriors. The still operational Roberts Drug Store on one corner looked like it had been there for years, but for the most part what had once been a busy little town now seemed one step away from becoming an empty façade for a Depression-era movie. Many of the buildings were long deserted, but several were occupied by businesses the structure obviously hadn't been designed for. To me, it looked like downtown was experiencing revitalization. I hoped so.

One block from the drug store was a building that obviously was once a grocery store but which now held the Out Of The Blue Flea Market. A bank building was the current home of a tiny local television station. A generic gray building with a wide white awning was Holder's Bail Bonds. Then there were the pink exteriored Brilliance Beauty Salon and an old feed store—there was an old sign on the side—the Re-Treat Thrift Store. All plain, all functional, all saturated with the feel of history.

Thomas's Furniture was fancier. The red brick building had a green awning, and the door and window shutters were cream and green. Nicely done. I got a picture of it as something tickled in the back of my brain.

Wait a minute, *Thomas*. That was Henry's store.

Getting across the road was easy, there were very few cars traveling down Main Street. I pulled open the door and walked into a small, typically laid out furniture story. Couches, chairs, tables, lamps, were all arranged in rough living room configurations. The colors were mostly basic, with a few old lady prints to round things out. The styles tended toward classic and seemed to be sturdy, well made pieces. I was impressed.

"Hi, I'm Ronny; could I interest you in a sofa today? There's a special offer this month: buy a sofa, get a free coffee table."

Ronny was in his late teens to early twenties, nice suit, tie, dark hair, big eyes, big smile. I kinda felt sorry for him. Poor guy, thinks he's got a live one on the hook, and I'm not even a minnow.

I gave him my best heartbreaker smile. "Actually, I'm wondering if Henry might be here."

I gotta hand it to Ronny; his smile wavered but didn't vanish. "He's in the back. I'll get him." He waved his hand. "Feel free to look around."

Sure I was free to look around. Free to find something that would make somebody—Ronny—a commission. I felt that twinge of guilt again.

"Stephie, it's good to see you."

I smiled at the sound. "It's good to see you too, Henry."

He hugged me, and I felt myself stiffen for a moment in surprise. I recovered pretty fast though, and hugged him back. I liked this man. Maddie could do worse for a step.

Henry let me go and moved back a bit, still smiling warmly. "So what brings you to my place?"

"I was walking around town and saw your sign." I shrugged. "I wanted to check out your store."

He raised one eyebrow. "Just wandering around town, huh?"

"I was avoiding a cheerleader brunch."

His lips twitched. "Well, I can understand that. Would you like a cup of coffee?"

"I'd love one."

He motioned toward the back, and I sat at a small table in a tiny break room. He handed me a Styrofoam cup with a wonderful smell coming from it, and I sipped at some truly delicious coffee.

Ronny stuck his head in the door. "Henry, unless you need me for something I'm going to run that bedroom suite out to the Holsoms."

"Ronny, come here and meet Stephie. She's a friend of Madison's, all the way from Washington, D.C."

"Nice to meet you, Stephie."

He had a firm, businesslike handshake. I was impressed. Henry apparently knew how to choose employees. "Nice to meet you too, Ronny."

He grinned at me for a moment, then seemed to shake himself and turned toward Henry. "I'd better get that delivery made."

"Tell Barbara I said hi."

"Will do." Ronny grinned my way and then headed out the door.

"He's a good kid," Henry said.

"He seems like it."

"I hope you enjoyed yourself last night."

"I did. The dancers were adorable. Women of the Hills is an amazing group, and that young singer was incredible."

Henry's lips twitched again. "And what did you think of the UFO?"

"Unexpected." I bit my lip to keep from smiling. "Does that sort of thing happen often around here?"

"No, but there've been sightings since the Seventies."

"Do you believe it might be a hoax?"

He chuckled as he leaned back. "Aliens, natural phenomena, or hoax, it sure makes life more interesting."

"Ever see a Bigfoot?"

For a man who had no problems with UFOs, he sure got his face bunched up in a hurry over the mention of a furry critter. All of a sudden he felt the need to go for more coffee.

"No, can't say I have," he said with his back to me.

When he turned back around, there was a smile on his face, though the creases at the corners of his eyes seemed more pronounced. "Would you like another cup?"

"I'm fine thanks. Actually, I think I need to get going. I have more exploring I want to do before the cheerleaders finish whatever weird stuff cheer-types do at brunches." A shudder flew through my body.

Henry chuckled. "I never trusted 'em much myself."

"Me either," I told him. "I preferred the guys who hung out in the library."

"I know what you mean. Back in high school, I spent many lunch hours in the library discussing science, science fiction, and whatever else crossed our minds."

My smile widened as a warm feeling of understanding grew in me. Henry was a lot like me. Well, me if I was a middle-aged, balding male who owned a furniture store. But still, I felt an affinity with him. "Thanks for the coffee."

He walked me to the door. "I'm glad you came by, hon. Stop by again before you leave. You hear?"

"I'll do that." Before I knew what I was doing I planted a kiss on his leathery cheek.

Embarrassed, I pulled back, but Henry was smiling. I waved goodbye and headed out. Such a sweet man. But then, Maddie's mom saw something she liked in him, and something told me she was a good judge of character.

Outside, the difference between the air conditioned

store and the sauna had me thinking about taking Henry up on that coming back to see him thing. Very soon. Like now, maybe.

I want to explore the town, I reminded myself. Besides, I was born a Southern girl. Just because I'd been living in Yankee territory for a while didn't mean my body couldn't re-acclimate to the weather—or at least that's what I kept telling myself as I headed down the sizzling street.

The county courthouse and grounds took up its own block. I smiled as I remembered the cool music, and yeah, the UFO. I couldn't help myself. It was interesting, even if the photos I'd shot didn't really show anything clearly enough to identify. Maybe the thirty-five millimeter film would show up something when I got back home and developed those shots, but I had my doubts. It was a mystery, and I dearly love mysteries. I'm not good at solving them, mind you. But I love them nonetheless.

Across from the courthouse was a side road with several businesses. Misty Lane, the sign said. One two-story, red brick building had my breath catching in my throat. The wooden sign hanging outside said Blackwood Antiques. He had invited me. But it would be disrespectful to my very closest friend to enter the lair of her enemy. Right? On the other hand, I could do some poking around in there. If Maddie had such a problem with this dude, he likely had some serious secrets hidden away. Maybe I could discover one or two. Give Maddie some ammunition to work with, in case she wanted to blackmail him or something. Yeah, that sounded legitimate.

I headed in the shop's direction, and when I saw

the beautiful things in the window, I added another reason for going in to my list: the possibility of a bargain. After all, I was the queen of haggling. I'd be willing to bet I could get a great deal out of one Jake Blackwood or his pimply teenaged employee.

I opened the door, and my heart kicked into high gear.

No dusty junk cluttered Jake's shop. This store was neat, clean and organized. Beautiful old furniture sat in key spots, surround by display areas showing off classic tools, gorgeous china, heavy silverware, and travel chests that looked like something Jane Austen might have used. There were old, but pristine, magazines. And cameras.

Of course, I headed straight to the camera section. A 1970s' Polaroid, an early Kodak, the body of an old Nikon and its once expensive, but now scratched, telescopic lens. Very cool.

An old Brownie made me smile. My father had a camera just like that. He told me it had belonged to his father and one day it would be mine. Of course, the camera, like everything else of his, had disappeared. A familiar heavy feeling pulled at me.

"Stephie. How nice to see you."

The voice had me jerking around in surprise. "Mrs. Clark?"

She smiled. "For goodness sake, call me Margaret. You're staying in my house, and I've heard so much about you from Maddie I almost feel like you're part of the family."

I tried to smile, to cover my inner wince. "What are you doing here?"

So much for diplomacy.

Mrs., um...Margaret chuckled. "I work here."

My head spun and I put up a hand to hold it together. "You what?

She put a hand on my shoulder and led me toward the sales counter. "I've been working for Jake for a little more than a year. I haven't told Madison yet. I figured my dating Henry was enough shock for the time being." She looked me straight in the eye. "I do intend to tell her though."

"Don't worry, your secret is safe with me." No way in hell I'm touching that little piece of info. Margaret can tell her daughter all by herself. After all, Maddie isn't likely to strangle her own mother barehanded.

"Thank you, Stephie. I appreciate your discretion." She indicated a chair and I took a seat. "Would you like some coffee?"

I'd really like something with more mind-numbing ability, but if coffee was what was available, I'd take it. "Yes, thank you."

"So what are you doing downtown alone?"

"Maddie had a cheerleader thing, so I thought I'd check out the town." I looked around again. "Jake has a nice place."

"Yes, he does, and he's quite proud of it." Margaret smiled, and pride filled her eyes. "He works very hard."

"It looks like it."

A door opened somewhere, and Jake walked in from the back storage room carrying a stack of boxes. He shot me a big grin. "Well hello, Stephie. Welcome to my store." He set the boxes down behind the counter and walked over to us.

"I think I'll take a break," Margaret said, as she sat

a cup of coffee in front of me then hurried off through the same door Jake had just used.

Great. Now I was alone with the enemy.

What was that underhanded reason I had for coming in here? Something about kissing... I mean gathering information?

"Well, what do you think?" he asked.

That you're gorgeous? Oh, wait, he means the store. "I think you have good taste." And I'll bet you taste good too. Oy!

He grinned, and I grinned back. Mentally I was kicking myself for being so nice to him. I was flirting with the enemy. Literally. Crap!

I leaned back in the chair and forced my face into an expressionless mask, or at least that's the look I was going for. "So, Maddie's mother works for you."

"Yes, she does, and I'm incredibly lucky to have her. Margaret's an amazing woman."

"And she's Maddie's mother."

His eyes clouded, just before he looked away. "Yes."

"And you don't feel guilty about that?"

Dark anger flared in his eyes when he looked dead into mine. "I have no reason, at all, to feel the tiniest bit guilty."

I held his gaze, and he didn't flinch. For a long, searing moment, I felt what seemed to be pent up rage. Then he looked away.

"What happened?" I could barely hear my own voice.

His gaze met mine again, but his expression was more guarded this time. "Didn't she tell you?"

"Maddie rarely talks about what happened when

her father died." I put a little extra emphasis on the last two words, and I saw him flinch. He didn't look away though.

"It was hard for me too," he whispered, then turned and moved to the far end of the counter. He poked through papers and moved things around a moment before he finally looked my way. "You'll have to ask her why she did what she did. I've tried to figure it out for ten years, and I keep coming up blank."

I stood and put my cup on the counter. "I need to go. I'm meeting Maddie."

"See you around." He didn't meet my gaze.

I headed out, more confused than before. And wondering what the heck I was going to do for the next two hours.

I wandered the streets for a while, getting a handle on the layout of the town. The thing is, the downtowns of most small Southern towns look alike. The same sort of buildings, the same narrow streets, the same sidewalks. But I had to admit, Ugly Creek had a different kind of feel to it, sort of a tingle. Or maybe the heat's cooking my brain. Maybe I should find some cool before I fry something I need.

I saw the sign, and I just had to check it out. Who could resist a place called the Arcane Restaurant and Magical Supply Shop?

Instead of the normal bell announcing my arrival, the opening door greeted me with the sound of tinkling wind chimes.

"Welcome," a male voice said, holding out his hand. "I'm Roy, I recognize you from the reunion. You're a friend of Madison's aren't you?"

"I'm Stephie. Wow, you have a good memory."

And a nice, strong handshake.

"To be honest, I might not have remembered if you hadn't been with Madison. She's kinda the unofficial star of our shindig this year."

"Because of her dad." Emotion filled my throat, and I had to swallow. "So you know Maddie?"

"Kind of." Roy looked at his shoes. "Back in high school, I didn't exactly run in the same crowd she did."

"Cheerleaders weren't exactly the kind of kids I ran with either."

He looked at me, and we shared a not-a-popular-kid bonding moment.

"We have some really great fried chicken today. And we have a special on incense, if you'd prefer to shop."

And once again I was in a store I wasn't planning on buying anything in. At this rate, I'll probably be reincarnated as a cheerleader. "I'm actually just looking around town, sightseeing basically."

"You aren't the first Yankee to poke around our little town. You're welcome to look around, and of course you must get your free Tarot reading from Connie."

"Oh, I didn't bring my nametag." How's that for a quick excuse?

"You don't need that. I saw you there." He took a couple of steps toward the counter in what was apparently the mystical supply section of the place. "Connie, got a minute?"

"Absolutely." The young woman came toward us, her brilliant red hair brushing her shoulders as she walked.

"This is Stephie," Roy said. "She's a friend of a

classmate of mine."

Connie smiled at me. "So you'd like a Tarot reading."

"I…I'm not sure."

"Trust me, you'll enjoy the experience."

Oh, what the hell? I followed Connie, and I couldn't help thinking she didn't look anything like a psychic. Thin, pretty, wearing jeans and a light blue top, she looked more like a college student than an expert in the occult.

She sat me down at a small, round table, and took the seat across from me.

"I have to tell you, I don't believe in this Tarot stuff."

Connie spread a red velvet cloth on the table and laid a deck of cards in the middle of it. "Honestly, I didn't believe in Tarot either until I started reading them."

Maybe the sun really had cooked some of my brain cells. "Why would you start reading cards if you didn't believe in their power, or whatever?"

The young woman's gentle, tinkling laugh was relaxing. "I was a bit of a rebel back in high school," she said. "Whatever would upset my parents appealed to me. I dressed in black clothes, dyed my hair a different color every week, bought pentacles and anything else that would freak them out. One day, I saw a gorgeous set of Tarot cards on the Internet and I bought them. It was supposed to be one more poke at my folks. Turned out, I was the one freaked by the things. The cards felt good under my fingers, like they were supposed to be mine. I did the spread like it said in the little booklet that came with them. And when I turned the cards over, I saw my life laid out before me. I've been working with Tarot ever since."

"Are the cards ever wrong?"

"No. But my interpretation is sometimes."

"That doesn't make sense."

"I'm going to shuffle until you tell me to stop." She smiled as she worked. "The cards give us the information; it's up to us to interpret it."

"Now."

She nodded, then spread out the cards, facedown, in an odd pattern. When she finished she turned over one card. "This is your past. The card is—"

"Don't tell me the names of the cards and all that, please. I'd prefer to just hear the weird news straight."

"Okay." Instead of being insulted, like I was afraid of, she chuckled. Then she turned over more cards, and her smile vanished. "Your past shows pain and betrayal; also the leaving behind of something important." She continued turning over cards. "Your present includes hard work, skill, and success."

All right, the woman seemed to hitting the right notes, but she might have been reading my expression, or even just guessing. I'm not a believer, okay, Aunt Octavia notwithstanding.

The way Connie tipped her head to the side and frowned slightly had me wondering if she was trying to come up with something believable—or seeing something weird. Wait a minute, crap! "Is that the death card?"

"That's the common name for it, but it usually doesn't mean death. In fact, in this case it definitely means change."

"Change?"

"Change, decisions, the ability to see hidden truths—and the potential for love." She grinned. "You have a very interesting spread."

"Um, thanks, I guess." Decisions again?

"It's good, I promise."

Apparently the "spreading" was over, so I stood.

"I'm really interested in how things turn out. Do me a favor and let me know." She handed me a business card.

"I'll do that." I turned to go.

"I'm serious," she said. "Your life is about to change."

"Hopefully for the better."

"That's up to you," she said, then turned her attention to picking up her cards.

As I headed out to meet Maddie, my head spun with the weird psychic stuff. First Octavia, now Connie. I was looking forward to hearing how the brunch went. How weird was that?

Maybe after lunch I could talk Maddie into going back to her mom's and relaxing for a while. I knew there was something planned for tonight, but she wouldn't tell me what. What were the odds I could get out of going? Slim to none, probably.

I took a deep breath and pulled open the door to The Café. So my spread was interesting, huh. Great. What was that saying? May you live in interesting times. Wasn't that a Chinese curse?

Chapter 6

I never in a gazillion years would have thought I'd attend a beauty pageant. But that's not the weirdest part. See, the kicker is that I was enjoying myself. How's that for about as strange as it gets? Of course, it helped a lot that most of the contestants only came up to my waist and none of them were old enough to drive.

The Little Miss Ugly Creek Pageant was held two days before the official Miss Ugly Creek Pageant. You know, the kind with the eye scratching, hair pulling young women putting their half-naked bodies out there to win fame, fortune, and college scholarships.

*Whatever.*

Tonight, though, was about little girls. Ranging from three to twelve years old, they were adorable. Yes, there was some eye scratching and hair pulling going on behind the scenes, but for the most part it wasn't the contestants—it was the mothers who behaved badly. I pointedly ignored that crap and took some awesome pictures of the most beautiful little girls in the world.

One of them had long, blonde hair and was dressed in a pink and purple fairy princess dress. She reminded me a lot of the pictures I'd seen of Maddie when she was a child.

I couldn't believe a pageant could actually be so much fun. I shot pics and enjoyed myself immensely. The event took place in the high school auditorium, and a couple of nearby classrooms were set aside as prep areas for the smaller girls and their parents. The older girls used the actual dressing rooms for privacy. I was heading toward the second of the classrooms when I heard a voice.

"Hello, *Buffy*."

Hearing my real name was bad enough. Hearing it in *that* voice made my skin crawl. Maybe he was talking to someone else. Yeah, someone else, that was the explanation. I'd ignore him and he'd go away.

And then Butch was in my face. "It's no use pretending that isn't your name," he said, leaning close enough I could smell his expensive aftershave. "I'm not stupid, you know. I know how to use the Internet. Your name is Buffy and you're from Alabama. Crooked Tree Hollow, Alabama, to be exact."

I stared into washed-out brown eyes. Eyes that held scorn, annoyance, and lust. His lips pulled into a smile that sent my insides rolling around with revulsion.

I wanted to run to the nearest airport and fly back to D.C. as fast as the first flight out could take me. But that would only be playing into his hands, as would denying the truth. I gave him the glare I used to aim at my stepfather. "So. What about it?"

A bit of his arrogance seemed to slip. "You're pretending to be some big old famous Yankee, when you're just as Southern as the rest of us. I'll bet you grew up in a trailer park, didn't you?"

I physically felt the power shift toward my side of the equation. "Buying into stereotypes only makes you look dumb. For your information, I may be Southern, but I was never poor. Ever."

I flashed my biggest, brightest smile, spun on my

heel, and headed down the hall to take pictures of a gorgeous little girl with obvious Asian genes. She had on a lacy lavender dress embellished with tiny embroidered pink roses. The child was absolutely adorable. Out of the corner of my eye, I saw Butch glaring. Then he turned and stomped out of the room. I took a big sigh of relief and focused on my shots.

While I worked I wondered what had crawled up and died in his pocket, and why I seemed to be the focus of his vexation.

I wondered what his next move would be. Because I knew for sure, this was far from over.

Two hours later, the pageant was in full swing, and I had all but forgotten Butch and his weird obsession with me. The little girls were cute, their talent segments were amazing, and I couldn't wait to see who won.

"Isn't this just the most fun in the world?"

Maddie's enthusiastic smile was contagious, but I managed to hold mine back. "It's not so bad."

She turned up her perfect little nose. "You just don't want to admit how much you're enjoying yourself."

Actually, there was some truth to that, but I'd be damned if I was about to admit to it. "This beauty stuff is more your thing than mine."

She wrapped an arm around my shoulders. "It's okay, I won't make you admit how great a time you're having."

Giggling, the little rat wondered off to do her bit helping with the miniature beauty queens. I allowed my smile to emerge as I turned back to picture taking. She knew me far too well.

The time passed faster than I would have believed,

and soon it was time for the climatic naming of the little winners. I noticed most of the kids got some sort of award, and all of the contestants got a ribbon and a certificate of participation. Whoever put this thing together seemed to have a real interest in making everybody happy.

Once the queen, cute little dark-haired Jodie Alonzo, was crowned, the crowd immediately went into a frenzy. Most of the parents and grandparents told the kids how well they'd done, but there were a few exceptions. A particularly harsh voice bellowed his kid would have won if she'd sang a little louder and had a better dress. The voice sounded familiar, so I peeked around the corner of the backstage area. Sure enough, it was my old friend Butch T. Jerk.

"She sings fine, and I could have got her a better dress if you would've given me more money, you stingy bastard." The woman, probably his wife, stood a foot from Butch's face and screamed right back at him.

"I ain't made of money, you know."

"Well, if people didn't know what you did, you might get a better job."

Butch's face went blood red. "I didn't have anything to do with that."

"Why do so many people think you do, then?"

"How the hell should I know?"

I turned off the flash and clicked a couple of stealth photographs. I had no idea what I'd do with them, but it seemed advisable to take advantage of the opportunity.

I caught both adults' angry expressions, and the teary-eyed face of the little girl who was begging them to stop. My heart went out to her, and I wanted so badly to comfort her, to take away her pain, that I took a step in their direction.

Realizing what I'd done, I quickly retreated around a corner where I wouldn't be seen.

The sound of footsteps shot a quick burst of apprehension through my chest. But it was the little girl who stomped around the corner, her lacy pink dress bouncing with each hard step. Her head was down, her tiny fists where clenched, and every few steps she'd swipe at the tears dripping off her cheeks.

"Are you all right?"

She stopped and stared at me. "Who are you?"

"My name's Stephie. I'm taking pictures of the pageant for an article my friend is writing."

She leaned her head to one side as if she was considering my words.

I gave her my best smile. "What's your name?"

"Lexie." She scrunched up her little face. "I hate my mom and dad."

"No, you don't."

She could glare hard for a little girl. "Yes I do."

"Okay. Why do you hate them?"

"Because they argue all the time." Tears began to flow again, and she swiped at her face with one fist.

"I'm sorry, Lexie. Sometimes adults yell." Boy, wasn't that the truth. "Just try to ignore them."

"They're yelling because I didn't win the pageant. I'm glad I didn't win. I hate the stupid pageant stuff."

"Why?"

"Because it's silly."

I sat on my heels and wiped a tear streaking down her face—and taking makeup with it. Foundation on a six-year-old. Freaky. "Your mommy and daddy want people to see how pretty you are."

"I don't want to be pretty. I want to be an astronaut."

I bit back my smile. I doubted she would understand it was because I understood her. "You can be both."

She blinked. "Mommy says I can't."

A flash of anger all but cooked my stomach. "Did she say why?"

"She said pretty girls should use what they have and not try to be smart too."

"You should meet my friend Madison, she's beautiful, and an award-winning journalist."

"Really?"

I made an X on my chest. "Cross my heart."

She leaned her head to one side again, as if contemplating my words. "You're pretty. And you're a picture taker."

I gotta admit a tear or two burned in my eyes. "Thank you."

"What are you doing with my kid?"

Uh oh, the jig was up. I stood and stared right into Butch's washed out, not-too-bright, anger-filled eyes. "I was talking to Lexie about being an astronaut."

He made a scoffing snort sound. "Girls can't be astronauts."

"Tell that to Sally Ride," I said.

I saw his frown of confusion as I walked away. Stupid idiot. I hoped with all my heart Lexie managed to ignore the backward thinking of her parents and live the life she was meant to live.

Twenty minutes later, everything was pretty much over. Contestants and their families were leaving and some of the staff began to take down the decorations

Cheryel Hutton

and such. I clicked a few quick shots as I wondered where Madison was. I knew she'd be wired for hours, but I was ready to go sit on the back porch, sip tea, and look for furry critters.

Remembering what I'd seen sent a wave of the jitters through me, but I was curious as hell anyway. Especially after the way Henry had reacted. What in the world was going on in this strange little town?

"I would have never pictured you at a kid's beauty pageant."

I spun, caught my foot on a thick black electrical cord, and almost fell on my butt. Jake's rock-hard arms caught me, and I stared up into his handsome face. I probably looked like an idiot, but I didn't so much care at the moment.

"Are you all right?"

I shook off the lingering stupidity and managed a smile. "I'm fine, thanks for catching me."

He grinned, and I all but swooned. "My pleasure."

We stood centimeters apart, our bodies aligned, our gazes locked. My heart beat faster, my breath came more quickly. I wanted to grab him and pull him closer. I wanted him to kiss me until I melted in his arms.

He leaned closer and hope rose like a balloon in a bright, sunny sky. Meanwhile, my conscience prodded me with a sharp stick. My very best friend had a problem with this guy. I had absolutely no business having the hots for him.

His lips touched mine, and I decided Maddie could fend for herself.

He pulled away and took a step back. "I'm sorry, Stephie."

I wanted to say something smart and pithy and

funny. But all I could think of was *play it again, Jake*. I'm such an idiot.

A beautiful redheaded woman sidled up to Jake and I had an insane moment of jealousy. "You about ready to get out of here?" she asked.

"Stephie, this is my sister, Valerie. Val, this is Maddie's friend from D.C."

"Nice to meet you."

I shook her hand. Sister. I will not admit to a wave of relief. Nope.

"Valerie's daughter was in the pageant." He pointed to a cute redhead talking with another of the contestants.

"She's adorable," I said, because she was.

"Thank you," Valerie said, her face beaming with motherly pride. "I think she might have won if I'd been willing to put makeup on her and spend five hundred dollars on a dress and take her to classes and stuff like the other mothers. But good grief, she's six! I wanted to do my bit to support the town, and to give Sienna the experience of a pageant, but I refuse to be a stage mother."

I liked this woman better all the time. Why was it I should be running in the other direction?

"Stephie."

And then I remembered.

I turned. "Maddie. Do you know—"

"Of course I do," she snapped. "I'll be in the car."

I watched her retreating back, while shame filled me with icy regret. What had I been thinking?

"Nice to meet you," Valerie said, then turned and hurried toward her daughter.

"I'm sorry."

I faced Jake. "It's not your fault. She's my friend."

"She used to be mine." I saw the flare of pain and regret in his dark eyes just before he turned and rushed after his sister.

I took a deep breath, turned toward the door, and hoped I had all my body parts when Maddie was through with me.

The parking lot was quickly emptying and Maddie's Aveo was easy to spot. She'd pulled closer to the building, and the motor was running. I jumped in and she took off before I had my seatbelt fastened.

Instead of taking the opportunity to chew me out, she was totally quiet on the ride back to her mother's house. I probably should have been grateful, instead I was worried. I figured the odds were excellent she was plotting my demise. If I was lucky.

Back at Margaret's, Maddie rushed up the stairs as if Bigfoot himself was after her. I chose not to follow. Instead, I wandered into the living room where Margaret sat on the couch reading a book. She smiled. "Did you enjoy yourself?"

"I did." I cringed. "Until Maddie caught me talking to Jake and his sister."

Margaret shook her head in sympathy. "I'll bet that went over like a gorilla at a formal state dinner."

"Pretty much." I sighed long and hard.

Margaret patted the seat beside her. "Wanna talk?"

I collapsed onto the couch, suddenly completely, utterly, exhausted. "I'm so confused."

"So you met Valerie? She's a sweet person."

"She seems to be. And her daughter is adorable."

Margaret smiled. "She's a good mother. Was her husband there?"

"I don't really know. Nobody introduced me to a guy, but then Maddie came up and everything got severely uncomfortable."

"He was probably at the hospital. Casey is an emergency room physician. We're all very proud of him."

I cringed. "Except Maddie."

"Madison isn't thinking straight."

"What happened between Jake and Maddie? Why does she hate him so much?"

Margaret stood and slowly walked to the doorway. She glanced up the stairway before sitting beside me again. "You have to understand, the fire scarred both of them, in different ways. You know Jake got trapped in the building, right? Virgil had to carry him out."

My stomach twisted painfully at the thought of what he must have gone through. "I knew he'd been hurt in the fire. I didn't realize..." I looked away, reluctant to let Margaret see the tears well up in my eyes.

"Both of them have deep scars. Some of Jake's are on the outside, but it's the scars we can't see that hold them both hostage to the events the night of the fire. Until those wounds start to heal, nothing is going to change."

I was sorry for both of them, but I was also confused. "But why do they hate each other?"

"They don't. Not really. My theory is that to each of them the other represents what they lost in the fire."

"That doesn't make sense."

"Not to you and me. And probably not consciously even to them. But deep down inside, neither of them has ever really dealt with what happened that night."

"The subconscious is a strange animal."

Margaret chuckled. "So are the two of them."

I had to agree. "I guess I'd better go face the firing squad."

"Good luck."

"Thanks. I'm pretty sure I'll need it."

I took a long, deep breath, and headed up the stairs."

Maddie was sprawled on her stomach across her bed; she had a mystery novel in her hand and appeared completely caught up in the story. She might have convinced me, if the book hadn't been upside down. All but overwhelming pain for my friend rushed through me. "Maddie, I'm sorry."

She shrugged without looking at me. "For what, talking to a guy you obviously like? Don't let me get in your way."

I cringed at the hurt and anger in her voice. "It's not that I like him."

She swung around and glared hard. "Yeah, you hate him, right? That's why you were kissing him."

Oh God, she'd seen. "He kissed me."

"Well that's different."

I took a step toward my friend. "Maddie, please..."

"Bite me, Buffy."

She flipped off the bed and tore down the hall. The bathroom door slammed.

I looked down to make sure I was still in one piece. The visual inspection insisted I was, but I was pretty dang sure she'd pulled out a piece of my heart. Maybe I should just pack up and head back to where I belong with my tail between my legs. I came to Ugly Creek to support my friend, and all it took was one, big, handsome man to have me acting like a seventh grader and leaving my best friend behind. What a jerk I was turning out to be.

I wandered over to the shelf of trophies and photos. Maddie as the head cheerleader. What a thud upside the head. Beauty, brains, and popularity. What did she see in short, crazy-haired, easily distracted me?

One thing was absolute. I would stay away from Jake Blackwood. We would only be in town for a few more days. I could certainly contain my hormonal overdrive for that long.

As I was sighing pitifully and turning to go have myself a kick-my-own-butt party, I realized there was another framed photo behind one of the entire cheerleading squad. I pulled it out and was greeted with Maddie in a prom dress, standing beside her date—Jake in a tux.

Oh boy. That explained a lot. No wonder there were such hard feelings between the two of them. Nothing creates more anger than lost romantic love.

Oh boy, my best friend, the closest friend I'd ever had, the woman who'd saved my sanity when I first got the job in D.C., had romantic feelings for a man I was falling for.

Just one more reason—as if I needed one—to keep my grubby paws off tall, dark, and trouble.

Sigh.

Chapter 7

"Play ball!" the umpire yelled.

From behind the refreshment stand counter, I had a great view of the annual Big Foot Festival's charity softball game. Every year, local business people, their employees, and families got together to raise money for a good cause. This year, thanks to Henry, the money was going to the county's Children's Hospital. Maddie asked if I would be willing to help out, and I was more than happy to say yes. Just the fact she'd spoken to me long enough to ask made my heart a little less lead-like. I'd tried to apologize on the way to the ball field, but she asked I just forget the whole thing. I wouldn't, of course. She'd always been there for me, and I'd been a horrible friend. I was lucky she was even speaking to me.

"Hot dog with everything, please."

I looked up into the dark, enticing eyes, and wanted to beat my head against the counter. I knew there was a good chance Jake would be at the game, but already? Good gravy.

"Coming right up," I managed, and turned to get his food.

"You were a lot friendlier last night."

Ouch. I fixed his dog and sat it on the counter between us. "Last night I wasn't thinking straight."

"Really."

I swallowed back the desire to crawl under the popcorn machine and forced myself to look at him. "Maddie is my closest friend."

He leaned near enough his hot breath brushed my cheek. "So, you're not even willing to get to know me before you toss me in the garbage. Figures."

He slammed money on the counter, snatched his dog, and stomped away. Perfect start to the day. Those two were going to be the death of me.

Luckily, before I could succumb to deep, dark, likely deserved, depression, a group of about a hundred loud, snotty nosed kids was nice enough to distract me. Okay, maybe it was more like five kids, but it seemed like a hundred. Even after they left, the need to scrub the entire area where they'd rubbed their grubby hands kept me busy for quite some time.

Two hours later, I'd pretty much forgotten grubby hands and irritatingly sexy men. The game was in full force, and I simultaneously enjoyed watching them play, and wished I was out there with them in the hot sun, hand curling around the ball, clutching the perfect heft of a bat, running headlong across the grass.

Maddie landed a solid hit on the ball and headed for first base. I felt warmth rush through me. My friend might be an ex-cheerleader, but she was also a decent athlete. Liza stepped up to the plate, and proved she could also handle a bat. Maddie scrambled for third and Liza slid into second. Jake stepped up to bat, and I held my breath.

The first pitch almost hit him in the leg. He jumped back and glared hard at the Stony Grove pitcher. He missed the next pitch, but he met the third pitch with the solid pop of his bat. The ball sailed high, arching over the heads of the opposing team.

Jake ran, Maddie ran, Liza ran. The crowd held its collective breath until Jake slid into home and Ugly Creek pulled into the lead. I did the Snoopy dance.

I heard footsteps and looked up to see Steve heading my way. "Having fun?"

"Yes, actually, I am." I did a bit more Snoopy. "That was an awesome play. Liza's an excellent athlete. You must be very proud."

"Yeah, I am." He grinned. "But her talents go way beyond softball."

I wasn't about to go down *that* road, so I changed the subject. "I didn't know Liza worked downtown." The game was between Ugly Creek downtown merchants, and the merchants of nearby Stony Grove. From what I'd picked up from overheard conversations indicated there were strict rules about who qualified.

"She doesn't, she works for me. Her father owns the hardware store, though. Since she's immediate family, she qualifies."

Liza stepped up to the pitcher's mound. Apparently she could not only hit the ball, she could pitch the dang thing too. My fingers twitched as if I were right there with her. "So, why aren't you playing?"

Steve laughed. "I hate to reinforce a stereotype, but I'm a computer geek. I'm not at all athletic."

"Too bad, softball can be a lot of fun."

"How about I take your word for it?"

"You're missing out, Zapata." My thoughts drifted to all the games I'd played. There was no feeling in the world like pushing your body to the limit and being part of a winning team.

A shriek had my breath freezing mid-inhalation.

Fear shot ice through my veins as I looked toward the field. Liza was still standing on the pitcher's mound, but she was doubled over. Then Steve was up and running, making his assertions about not being athletic into a lie. He was with his wife before I was even halfway there.

There was a tight knot of people around Liza, all of them talking at the same time. Steve shoved through. "What happened? Are you all right, sweetheart?"

"I'm so sorry," the guy who'd been up to bat was saying.

I finally managed to get close enough to see Liza was holding her right arm close to her body. "I'm all right, Steve," she said, though the tremor in her voice and the tears in her eyes told me she was in serious pain.

"Let's get you to the hospital." They started off, Steve's arm protectively around his wife.

"I'm going with them," Madison said, and proceeded to shove people out of the way so Steve and Liza could get through.

"We need you to take Liza's place!" the Ugly Creek coach protested.

"Stephie can do it," Maddie yelled back, as she hurried across the field with Steve and Liza.

Suddenly all eyes were trained on me. I gulped. This was obviously one of those instances where you need to be careful what you wish for. "It's been a long time since I played."

"We're desperate," Henry told her. "Will you do it?"

"Hey, wait a minute," the Stony Grove coach said. "She doesn't qualify."

Henry turned to face the man down. "Come on, George! The score's tied and we just lost two of our best players. It's a charity game!"

George, whose face started to turn bright red, said, "Unless she works downtown, or is immediate family of somebody who does, she can't play."

I saw Henry open his mouth, but before anything came out, Jake jumped in. "I need some extra help at the store."

I spun, wondering if this were some sort of trick to punish me. Jake met my gaze and held it.

"You can't just make up some excuse and pretend to hire her." George sounded decidedly unhappy.

"It's not an excuse," Jake said. "Stephie's a photographer and Ace is in California rescuing animals from the fire area. What about it, Stephie, I need to update my catalogue and my website, are you willing to take some photos for me?"

There was challenge in Jake's eyes, and I dearly loved challenge. "Sure. I'll work for you."

He held out his hand, we shook, and turned simultaneously to look at George. "Fine," he said, and stomped back to his dugout.

"I hope you know how to play softball," Jake whispered.

I just smiled and hurried off to our dugout to warm up. Somebody found an extra team T-shirt, and I pulled it on over my sleeveless blouse. The bright red team shirt looked hideous with my purple shorts, but at least I had on my trusty sneakers. The thought of running bases in sandals brought the word "horrifying" to mind.

Jake took the pitcher's spot, and though he wasn't as good as Liza, he wasn't bad either. I was sent to the outfield, probably where I could do the least damage, but it wasn't long before I returned a ball in time to prevent a runner from making it to third base. Our team worked hard, but the other team did manage to sneak one run past us. So the score was tied when we went up to bat.

Their pitcher was good, that's for sure. Our first batter quickly struck out. The second got to first base. The third batter also made it to first, but the other runner got tagged on the way to second.

Jake took the bat, and I held my breath. I didn't need to worry. He hit the first pitch and easily made it to second. The other runner was on third. And it was my turn.

I picked up the bat I'd chosen, adjusted the borrowed helmet, and got into position. The first pitch was way out of my range. The pitcher was testing me. The second came closer, but I still didn't attempt a swing. I just smiled at the pitcher.

The third pitch was damn near perfect, and I felt kinda like Wonder Woman when the bat connected and the ball flew toward the outfield.

I took off running for base. First, second, third, and they still didn't have it. I was heading for home when I suddenly realized the ball was back in play and heading my way. Without a thought, I dove for the ground and slid into base just before the ball hit the opponent's glove.

"Safe!" the referee yelled.

As I walked off the field to the sound of cheers, I saw Jake grin in my direction. Good intentions be damned, I was thrilled. The man might be a real jerk, but he was for-sure a sexy one.

I dusted myself off as I watched the next batter. The woman managed to hit the ball, but only made it to first, and then the final batter struck out.

The Stony Grove team went to bat, and I was assigned to third base. Apparently our coach had decided I could play after all.

The other team managed to get a player on first and second, but I had the honor of procuring an out as their second base runner tried for third. Their next two batters struck out, and the game was over.

Hugs and dancing and general festivities began, along with handshakes and well wishes to and from the other team. It shocked me to my toes when I realized I'd missed this part of small town life.

"Celebration at Pizza Town!" Henry yelled.

I wanted to go. I felt my eyes burn and my heart drop a little at the thought of going back to Margaret's house. I wanted to be part of the celebration, but I didn't fit in. I wasn't part of this life, of this world. I, after all, had made a conscious choice to leave this sort of thing behind.

Jake grabbed me by the arm and leaned close. "Don't even think about not going. You're the star of this party."

"No. I helped out; the rest of you did the hard work."

"We couldn't have done it without you. Come on." With a grip that was just this side of painful, he took me with him to a big green pickup parked toward the back of the lot. He pulled open the passenger door and I climbed in.

"I know you're a city girl," he said, as he slid into the driver's seat. "You've probably have never even been in a truck before."

"Actually, my dad had a pickup." Why had I said that?

"Let me guess, big, shiny, and new?"

I couldn't help but smile at the thought. "More like ancient and rusty and wouldn't run when it rained."

He looked at me, his eyes wide. "You're kidding."

I shrugged. "He loved the old thing."

"So, are you from D.C. originally?"

"Near there." If you could call eight hundred miles south "near."

"You're probably bored silly out here in nowhere land."

"No, I'm enjoying myself." Which was incredible, actually.

"I'm glad."

"Are you?"

"Why wouldn't I be?"

I poked at a big splotch of dirt on my right knee. "Because I'm here with Maddie."

He made a scoffing sound. "It's not your fault."

I felt my shoulders tighten and my breath pull in hard through my nose. "Just because the two of you can't get over something that happened ten years ago—"

"Look, if you keep on, I'll wind up saying something you don't like about your friend, and then you'll be mad. And then I'll get mad and the whole thing could get ugly. I'd really rather just enjoy the victory party."

I hated he was right, but he was. "Okay. I'll keep my big mouth shut."

Jake pulled his truck into the Pizza Town parking

lot, killed the motor, and turned to look at me. He stared for a moment, his eyes narrowed; his head leaned to one side. I was feeling distinctly uncomfortable. "Is there dirt on my face?"

"It isn't big."

"What?"

His lips twitched. "Just checking out your mouth. Not big, but pretty tasty, if you ask me."

With that, he opened his door, slid out, and headed toward the restaurant.

I jerked the door open and climbed out of the truck. Even running, I didn't catch him until he was almost at the door. "Rat," I told him as I swung past and pushed in before him. I was quite disappointed he grabbed the door before it slammed closed in his face. No wonder Maddie didn't like him.

Pizza Town was a bright family friendly place with red and white checked tablecloths, a real jukebox, and overworked waitresses who looked like it took every bit of strength they had to keep smiling. Still, they seemed genuinely happy to see us, and to hear their town's team had won.

Several tables were quickly shoved together to form one that stretched from the front of the restaurant to almost the back wall. I sat across from Margaret and Henry and smiled at the expression of love I saw on their faces. I took some quick shots of the group and made sure to get a clear pic of the two of them.

Someone sat in the seat next to me, and I knew even before I looked I wasn't going to be happy about it. "Isn't there somebody else you could harass?"

"Actually, I wanted to talk to you about the job. I was thinking you could ride to work with Margaret in the morning."

Margaret tightened her lips into a line. "Jake, the girl is on her vacation. Why don't you give her a break?"

"I'd hate to have our win rescinded on a technicality." He caught my gaze and held it. "Besides, I really could use your help."

Why did I think I was about to regret not going with Maddie and Liza to the hospital? "What exactly do you need me to do? You said something about taking pictures?"

"Actually, it should be right up your alley. I have a website and a brochure I like to keep up-to-date. It isn't, and the guy who usually takes the pictures is in California doing his animal rescue thing. Now, I could get my trusty cheapo camera and do some shots, but it wouldn't look very professional. The only other option is to wait for Ace to get back, which is what I was going to do. I'm not happy with either option. And that's where you come in."

Well, if it involved taking pictures of antiques, maybe it wouldn't be so bad after all. He seemed to have some pretty nice things in his shop. "Okay, I'm in." I looked at Margaret. "What time do you leave for work?"

"Seven-thirty."

Yikes!

"Margaret," Jake said, "you don't have to be there so early. Why don't you two come in at ten?"

"Oh, no. I don't want to mess up your schedule," I said. "It's not a problem. I'll be ready at seven-fifteen tomorrow morning." Ready for what, I wasn't sure.

Margaret shrugged. "Whatever."

The waitress got to our section, and the next few minutes were spent debating how many different kinds of pizza to order. Personally, if it's got crust, tomato sauce, and cheese, I'm all over it.

The conversation turned to what the rest of the festival had to offer. I felt unexpected excitement as the people around me talked about music, crafts, a carnival complete with rides and games, and the parade that would be the high point of the festival. It had been a long time since I'd been part of a small town party and I was shocked at how much I was looking forward to the next few days.

Except, of course, the whole working for Jake thing. I wasn't looking forward to that. Really, I wasn't.

Time passed, the celebration began to break up, and suddenly I realized Henry and Margaret weren't across from me any longer.

I turned to Jake. "Did they leave?"

"Who?"

"Margaret and Henry."

"They took off about five minutes ago," the first-baseman said.

*Great.* "I was counting on Margaret for a ride back to her house."

"I'll take you," Jake said.

I closed my eyes for a moment, hoping the whole fiasco would just vanish. Unfortunately it was still there when I opened my eyes again. "Fine."

"Calm down, all that excitement isn't good for you."

I turned and gave him my very best glare. It should have backed him up a couple of feet. All it did was provoke a grin.

A few minutes later I was back in the green pickup, and Jake appeared to have decided he'd take me to Margaret's but he didn't have to speak to me. And just when I was beginning to think he might not be as big a jerk as I'd thought.

As much out of orneriness as curiosity, I brought up the one subject that seemed to get everybody's tails twisted. "So, Jake, have you ever seen a Bigfoot?"

The truck jerked, and for a moment I thought I had made the biggest—and possibly last—mistake of my life. He quickly got the vehicle under control, and I closed my eyes and breathed a prayer of thanks. Not that I'm a big religious-type person, but it seemed the thing to do under the circumstances.

"What in the world made you ask that?"

"Um, Big Foot Festival. You know, the reason I'm here."

"The festival is named in honor of the town founder. Didn't anybody tell you?"

"The guy with big feet. Yeah, I know. I was just making conversation."

Jake went back to being silent and I tried to think of something to say that wouldn't have him losing control of his pickup. "It sure is hot, isn't it?"

"Yep."

Before I could think of another topic of conversation, he pulled into Margaret's driveway and sat staring at her house open-mouthed. "It really is purple."

"You didn't know?"

"I never come out here." I saw him swallow hard. "Not anymore. I'd…um…I'd heard the house was purple, but I figured it was really blue or even some odd shade of brown. But it's really deep, vivid, dancing dinosaur purple."

"It's an awesome thing to do. Margaret has a wonderful sense of whimsy."

"Figures you'd like a purple house."

I leveled a narrow-eyed glare at him. "Yeah, what about it?"

"In case you haven't noticed, you're a little on the different side." He smiled, just a little smile, but it was enough to float my traitorous heart to the top of my chest.

"Different side of what?"

He brushed the back of his fingers gently across my cheek. "Pretty much everything."

I couldn't move. Not my hand, my leg, or even my lungs. I was frozen; unbreathing, unthinking, unbelieving of the warmth of his touch or the hot desire roaring deep in my abdomen. Hot and cold, ice and fire, loathing and lust.

Jake.

He pulled away and grabbed the steering wheel with white knuckle force. I knew I should take the opportunity to go, but I didn't want to.

I mentally kicked my own rear and pulled open the door. Before I headed to the house, I turned and spoke into the open window. "Thanks for the ride. I'll see you tomorrow morning."

He stared at nothingness as he said, "Maddie left for college right after high school graduation. I was still in the burn unit."

Before I could think of something to say, he put the truck in gear and started backing up. All I could do was jump back from the moving vehicle before I was knocked off my feet.

As I watched him roar away, I considered what he'd said, and the way his scar had blanched when he said it. It had to be all a big misunderstanding. There was no way the sweet, giving, loyal friend I knew could have anything to do with the agony I'd seen in Jake's eyes.

Right?

## Chapter 8

The front door was unlocked, so I opened it and walked into the house. I seriously needed a shower, but more than anything I needed to think.

I headed toward the stairs, but before I got beyond the first step I heard Margaret's voice from the living room. "You got home all right, I see."

It would be rude to ignore my hostess, so I stuck my head in the living room doorway. Margaret and Henry sat side by side on the couch.

"Jake brought me," I told them, feeling a bit of irritation with the two of them, especially when Margaret smiled.

"I knew he would; he'd never leave a woman stranded. He's such a sweetheart."

Sudden understanding smacked me in the face. *The rats!* "You left me there on purpose."

Margaret shrugged and motioned for me to have a seat across from the couch. "I just thought it'd be good for the two of you to have some time alone."

I perched on the edge of the chair, hoping I wouldn't get the beautiful fabric dirty, while I wondered what she could possibly mean. No way could it be what I suspected. "What, were you hoping we'll kill each other or something?"

Margaret laughed. "Not at all. In case you haven't noticed, Jake is quite taken with you. I was just, shall we say, giving things a bit of a prod."

That had me staring like a complete idiot. "Taken? With me? Huh?"

"You mean you really haven't noticed."

"There is some attraction. But," I hastened to add, "there are a lot of reasons for us to keep far apart."

"Like Madison?"

"Exactly."

Margaret sighed. "What's between Jake and Maddie is their problem, not yours."

"But she's my best friend. She rented me her extra room, she showed me the ropes in D.C., she took me to the hospital when I had appendicitis."

"Then it'll be your decision whether to follow up on your attraction. All I did was give you two a chance to connect." She shrugged innocently. "Besides, you and Jake will be working together. You might as well figure out how to get along."

Oh boy! What had I gotten myself into?

"I figure Jake doesn't know what to do with either one of 'em," Henry said.

"Really?" Margaret asked.

Henry nodded. "You have to understand; women are mysterious creatures to us men."

"I'm mysterious?" Margaret asked him.

"Sweetheart, you're the most mysterious woman I've ever met." He pulled her close and kissed her.

"I'm going to take a shower," I said, not at all sure the couple heard me. I smiled as I headed toward the stairs. There was nothing more wonderful in the world than the expression on the faces of a couple in love. Not just lust, or even the beginnings of true caring. The best love was that of a couple who'd gone past all that, of two people who cared enough about each other to risk lives, livelihoods, or even hearts. That was the kind of love I wanted to find. The kind I saw in Henry and Margaret's faces.

I'd just started up the stairs when the front door opened and Madison walked in. "How's Liza?" I asked.

"She cracked a bone in her wrist, but she'll be fine." Maddie grinned. "She's got Steve falling all over himself taking care of her."

I sighed. "So that's the secret. All you have to do is get hit with a softball and crack a bone."

Madison shuddered. "I'll just stay single."

"You and me both, sister."

Maddie started up the stairs. "I seriously need a shower."

"Hey, I was on my way to the shower first." I rushed up the stairs behind her.

"No way José! I've got hospital cooties on me." Madison swung up the last few steps, and slammed the bathroom door in my face.

"I'll remember this!" I yelled at her through the door.

"Be my guest," Maddie yelled back.

"I *am* your guest. And you should treat me better."

"Whatever." The shower turned on.

I went to gather clean clothes and hope there'd be hot water left when Maddie finished. The odds really weren't in my favor. Oh well, maybe a cold shower would get my mind off that annoying varmint by the name of Jake.

While I was waiting, I booted up my laptop and downloaded the pictures I'd taken at the game. I was smiling when Maddie came in the room wearing a soft pink bathrobe with a big blue towel wrapped around her head. She plopped down on the floor beside me. "Good pics."

"Thanks."

"I heard we won."

I smiled, remembering. "We did."

"Thanks for helping out."

"I enjoyed it."

She began drying her hair with the towel. "I knew you would."

"About that. There was a fuss because I wasn't an employee of a downtown business."

She shrugged. "I thought there might be. Did Henry give you a job or something?"

I stared hard at the computer screen. "Not Henry."

She sighed and got to her feet. "Let me guess. You're working with Mom at Jake's store."

I couldn't help it. I stared at her. "You know about that."

She combed out her long, blonde hair. "I've known for a while. I just don't understand why she didn't tell me."

"She thought her seeing Henry was enough to deal with for a while."

Maddie nodded. "I can see the logic in that. I wish she'd told me though. It was embarrassing to find out from that bitchy slut Kimmie Vaughn."

"I'm just taking pictures for Jake." She didn't say anything, so I continued. "Maybe I should tell him I can't do it."

She turned to glare at me. "And let Stony Grove yank away the win from us? Don't even think about it!"

"I don't want to cause any problems between you

and me."

"Working for Jake to qualify you to play softball is one thing." She looked at the comb in her hand. "Kissing him is something else entirely."

I held up my hands in surrender. "I'm just going to take photos of his stuff for his website and brochure. That's all."

She gave me a hard narrow-eyed glaring stab. "He's not a nice person."

"I get it."

She continued to scrutinize my face for a moment, then nodded. "Okay. I'm planning to do a bunch of stuff with the squad tomorrow anyway." She narrowed her eyes and gave me a you're-so-missing-out-but-whatever look. "I know you don't want to spend time with a bunch of ex-cheerleaders."

"Not so much."

"Still interested in the craft fair Friday afternoon?"

"Wouldn't miss it for the world."

She smiled and went back to untangling her shiny golden mane. I grabbed my stuff and headed for a cold shower.

****

I sat on the back porch again that evening, but I didn't see anything resembling a bear, Bigfoot, or Great Dane in a china shop. I did have an interesting conversation with a squirrel. Yeah, I said conversation, and no, squirrels in Ugly Creek don't speak English. At least I don't think they do.

This one came right up on the top step and stood there looking at me. I happened to be munching on some truly awesome peanut butter cookies á la Margaret, and I got the feeling that Mr. Squirrel thought

I was being pretty selfish. I tried to ignore him, but he pulled out his arsenal of cute, and I finally gave in and scooted a bit of cookie his way. He picked it up, stood holding it while looking at me, and I knew as well as if he'd spoken that he was telling me, "Just how am I supposed to feed my wife and kids with this tiny little piece."

I tried to explain cookies were fattening, but he only narrowed his cute little eyes. Finally I caved and slid a whole cookie across the porch. As soon as I did, I realized the creature wouldn't be able to carry such a huge bounty. That cookie was enormous compared to his tiny little body. I wondered if he would let me break it up.

He was gone. And so was the cookie. I'd been looking at him the whole time, apparently he'd moved when I blinked. I shook my head and chuckled at the whole episode. It seemed even the squirrels in this town were weird.

I picked up my plate and turned to go into the house. I'd opened the door when I heard a rustling behind me. I turned and squinted into the darkness, but I didn't see anything. Probably it was my buddy the cookie-mooching squirrel climbing a tree. Although it had sounded like a larger creature.

A bit spooked, I went into the house. I couldn't resist one last, lingering look out into the dark yard. I thought I saw movement by a huge oak tree, but when I didn't see anything else, I decided it had to be my imagination.

If there was a Bigfoot out there, he or she wasn't going to let me know about it.

A big yawn reminded me I had to get up early in

the morning, so I locked the door, rinsed my dishes, and headed up the stairs. I wasn't looking forward to seeing Jake. Really I wasn't. I just wanted to be ready for anything.

Because there's no telling what might happen in Ugly Creek.

Chapter 9

Madison was still in bed when Margaret and I headed to work. Margaret's car, believe it or not, was a red Mustang convertible. She called it her "bad girl" car and was obviously very proud. We rode with the top down, cool air sweeping over us, my wild hair getting wilder by the mile. It was so much fun I actually forgot momentarily I was headed to town to work for a sexy...I mean, an obnoxious, pain-in-the-backside man.

To keep that thought in check, I decided the drive time could be useful for uncovering long buried, but still fascinating secrets. "I'll bet Maddie was an interesting kid."

That's all it took to start the stories flowing. There were tales of stealth tree climbing and compulsory Barbie doll swapping, but the best was the one about the permanent marker tattoos Madison, Liza, and Jake gave each other on their faces and arms.

"It took weeks for the ink to wear off," Margaret said, laughing.

"Sounds like they had a lot of fun growing up," I said.

"It was almost like they were three parts of a whole," Margaret said. "It's a shame they're not close anymore."

That would have been the perfect opportunity to ask pertinent questions, but unfortunately we'd reached our destination and Margaret pulled her car behind the store into a lot I didn't even know existed. Jake's green truck was already there. Great.

Margaret used her key to unlock the back door, which led into a storeroom. A huge cappuccino-color dog that looked a bit like a retriever, but had definite German shepherd markings on his face, greeted us. "Good morning, Dingo," Margaret said, giving the dog a good head scratch. *Dingo?*

He came over to me, and I held out my hand so he could sniff it. Seemingly satisfied with what he smelled on me, Dingo flopped down at my feet.

I sat on my heels, and the dog rolled over onto his back. Laughing, I gave him the belly scratching he was so obviously asking for. One back leg thumped air, and the look on his face reminded me of Maddie when she ate Godiva chocolate.

"Oh great, somebody else to spoil the mutt."

I bit my lip to hold the smile down to a minimum. "He needed a belly scratch."

Jake sat on his heels on the other side of Dingo. "*Needed*, huh?"

"Yep."

Jake ruffled the top of the dog's head. "You're a con artist, Dingo."

"Maybe so," I said, "but he's a gorgeous one. Aren't you, boy?"

The dog licked my arm.

Jake laughed. "I give up."

I hate to admit it, but Jake's closeness was causing tingles in interesting places, like between my legs. I was a horrible friend. "How long have you had him?" I asked, and hoped to give myself a moment to beat my traitorous body into submission.

"About two years. A friend of mine, Ace, the guy who usually does my photography, rescues dogs. Anyway, Ace had this fellow. It was love at first sight, wasn't it, boy?"

Dingo licked his master's hand, and the smile that crossed Jake's face was pure affection. Okay, I'll admit I was just a hair jealous. Why can't I find a man who appreciates my touch?

I pulled myself to my feet. "Speaking of job, I guess I'd better get to mine."

Jake stood too. "Just let me take Trouble, I mean Dingo, upstairs and I'll show you what I need you to do. There's coffee if you want some."

I grabbed a Styrofoam cup of hot liquid, poured in a pack of sugar, and wandered out into the main area of the shop. Once again I was swept away by the displayed antiques. Beauty and history, what an amazing combination.

I set my cup down on the counter and went over to a nearby table where a beautiful china doll sat in a little, handmade wooden chair. With the very tips of my fingers I gently touched the doll's face. "Gorgeous," I breathed.

"She is, isn't she?"

I smiled toward Margaret, who sat on a stool at the counter and sipped her own cup of coffee. "Yes," I said. "She really is."

I went back to where I'd left my cup and climbed onto the other stool. "This place is incredible."

She smiled, and I saw pride in her eyes. "Jake has done quite well with his little store, in spite of everything."

Well, that had my curiosity jumping up and down. "Everything?"

She glanced toward the back before she answered. "Not only was he burned severely in the fire, his leg was crushed also. It was weeks before they even attempted to repair the damage, because he wasn't strong enough to withstand the surgery."

"Wow. He doesn't even have a limp."

"He worked very hard at physical therapy." She licked her lips. "Actually, he works hard at everything he does. Which of course, his father doesn't see."

"Really?"

She nodded. "His father is still upset Jake didn't use his business degree in some big prestigious firm. But he wanted to stay here in Ugly Creek and open his own shop."

There was a noise from the back, and we both turned to see Jake come into the shop carrying a big box. "Margaret, would you start inventory of the Barinski items while I show Stephie what I need her to do?"

"No problem, boss."

He sat the box on the counter and gave Margaret a kiss on the cheek. "You're a gem."

"Nah, I'm just a good gofer." She stuck her front teeth out in imitation of a gopher.

"You're not a gopher, you're a nut."

She grinned over her shoulder as she dug into the contents of the box.

Jake motioned for me. "Come on and I'll show you what I need photographed."

First up was a gorgeous chair with intricately carved armrests and legs.

I gently ran a finger over the polished wood. "Incredible craftsmanship," I whispered.

"You have a good eye. This chair was locally made in the late 1800s."

I sucked in air. "Are you serious?"

"Oh, I don't joke about things like that." His fingers caressed the edge where fabric met polished wood. "It hasn't even been recovered."

My heart and lungs stalled for long enough to make me see black spots. "That's the original fabric?"

He nodded. "This chair came from an estate sale. An old man passed away, and this chair was in the collection. From what his son told me, it had belonged to the old man's grandfather. It's certainly been well cared for."

I stared at him, feeling my eyes widen in utter disbelief. "The son didn't keep it?"

Anger passed over Jake's face. "I asked him if he was sure he wanted to sell it. He said it wouldn't work with his décor."

Paralyzing shock held me for a long moment, before tears inexplicitly filled my eyes. I looked toward the chair to keep Jake from seeing. "If I had this gorgeous piece, I'd build my décor around *it*."

A gentle hand touched my shoulder. "Me too. In fact, I'm considering not selling it."

Gladness filled my heart at the thought. He would care for the chair, enjoy it, treasure it. My fingers moved across the gently rough fabric.

"Of course, I want to keep a lot of things. I have to be pretty selective, or I'd have a house I couldn't walk through and an empty bank account."

I glanced his way. He was looking at the chair with

an expression of awe. I felt my heart connect with his. "If I owned a store like this, I'd have the same problem."

He gave me an odd little look, almost as if he'd forgotten I was there. "Go ahead and take pictures of the chair, and I'll make my mind up later."

I nodded, and he walked me around the store to show me the other history-laden treasures he wanted me to photograph. We barely looked at each other and our speech was professional and bland. I knew we were both fighting another connection like the one over the chair. Maybe if we were simply two people who happened to meet and bond over antiques, perhaps then things would be different. But life was complicated, so we forced ourselves to be distant and cool.

Until we got to the cedar chest in the corner.

Inside were the most beautiful clothes I've ever seen. There were two 1920s' flapper era dresses, one green and one black; a 1950s' white poodle skirt, with an actual poodle appliqué, and a timeless party dress in soft, lacy violet. That one had me gasping. Actually, I think I drooled a little.

"Like it, huh?"

I surreptitiously wiped my mouth. I couldn't resist holding the party dress up in front of me. "It's amazing." I glanced back at the other clothes. "All of this is."

It was quiet, so I glanced Jake's way. He was watching me; his head leaned slightly to one side, his expression soft, his lips turned up in a gentle smile. "You know, I don't usually handle clothing. The chest and contents came from an estate sale. I took it all, sight unseen."

I looked down at the soft fabric swirling around my legs. "What are you going to do with these?"

"I was going to find somebody to take them off my hands." His shoulders moved in an almost shrug. "You know, I could pay in merchandise."

It took a moment for the significance of his words to sink into my awe-soaked brain. "Pay? With *this*?" I held up the dress.

His smile widened. "Actually, I was thinking the chest and its contents."

Air sucked into my lungs and refused to go back out. "All of it?" I gasped.

"You'd actually be doing me a favor taking it off my hands."

Yeah, right, and the moon is mozzarella. But hey, if he was willing I wasn't going to complain. "Well, if it would be helpful."

The varmint actually chuckled. "Stephie, one of the best things about being an antiques dealer is seeing beautiful things find homes with people who will appreciate and enjoy them."

"Thank you," I whispered.

"Thank you for helping me with the pictures."

"You're welcome." As I stood looking at him, the warmth in his eyes radiated my body and sent feverish prickling up and down my arms. How could he have this effect on me? He wasn't a nice man. Maddie didn't like him.

Then again, her mother worked for him. And liked him. So, he couldn't be that bad. Could he?

Confusion swirled in my head. For a moment I wasn't even sure who I was. Where I was. What planet I was on?

What was that tinkling noise?

"Hello, Margaret."

"Good morning, Aunt Octavia. How are you?"

Oh boy. Margaret. She'd been right there all this time, watching me stare cow-eyed at her daughter's sworn enemy. And now Aunt Octavia was there too. What was I thinking? Actually, the answer was pretty simple. My brain was currently non-operational.

"I need to see Aunt Octavia," I blurted, and hurried toward the front of the store. What I saw had me frozen in mid-step. The cute, tiny, salt and pepper haired woman had turned into a miniature biker babe complete with boots, black jeans, a tie-dyed T-shirt, and a black leather jacket.

She waved her hand to indicate her clothing. "Do you like my outfit? I decided to ride my Harley today."

"You have a Harley?"

"Hell yes, there ain't no other bike."

My mouth worked like a fish gasping for water. "I mean...I..." Like I said, brain non-operational.

"Oh, my. Your auras are in tune."

She was looking at me, and behind me. Oh great.

"So what does that mean, Aunt Octavia?" Jake asked.

Granny Biker Babe smiled. "It means the two of you are destined for romance." She turned to Margaret. "Don't they make a cute couple?"

"Yes, they do." Margaret's smile was a little too smug.

I groaned. "Look, I know you really believe what you're saying, but there is no way the two of us..." I glanced behind me. "It's just not possible."

A smug little smile pulled at Aunt Octavia's bright

red lips. "I heard you almost got run over the other day. A green VW, wasn't it? Maybe a Rabbit?"

"I'll admit I can't explain that, and I don't mean any disrespect. But—"

"No buts. Ask Margaret. Ask anybody who's known me very long. I have the gift. It's God given, and it's never wrong."

She turned and started toward the door, only to stop in mid-step, freeze for a moment, then look over her shoulder. "Jacob, your mother says not to let your stubborn nature get in your way. You deserve happiness."

She left, and I stood staring at the door.

"I wish she wouldn't do that," Jake said. He turned and stomped off toward the back room.

"I should get to work taking pictures." I picked up my camera bag and headed toward the first piece.

As I worked, I kept glancing toward the back. What Aunt Octavia had said, and Jake's reaction to it, had me intrigued. Was Jake's mother dead? Margaret had only spoken of Jake's father. Her death would explain why she had to communicate with him through Aunt Octavia.

Whatever was going on, it certainly upset Jake. As sure as I was he had to have done something to upset Maddie, I still wanted badly to rush to him, to comfort him, to hold him in my arms, to kiss away the sadness, to pull him close, to feel his hands on my back.

Okay, getting way beyond the desire to comfort and headed straight into much more dangerous territory. Clearly my hormones were out of control.

Maybe that's what comes of a single, frequently dateless, woman lusting after the kind of relationships very few couples ever experience. It was ridiculous.

Jake came out of the back room and went over to the counter. He was flipping through papers so hard I expected the sheets to start flying through the air any minute. "Where's this month's inventory list? I know I had it yesterday. Damn it! I can never find anything around here."

Margaret stood and calmly went over to a filing cabinet, pulled a file out and handed it to him. "Exactly where you put it."

Jake closed his eyes for a moment, head down, the effort to get himself under control painfully obvious on his face. "I'm sorry, Margaret."

She leaned against the counter, arms crossed over her chest. "I think it might be a good time for you to take a break."

He nodded. "Dingo could use a walk."

He went toward the back, and a moment later I heard footsteps going up a flight of stairs. I'd suspected he lived above his business, and apparently I was right. That explained a few things. I fiddled with my camera for a few minutes, trying to get my thoughts back on my work.

There was the sound of footsteps coming back down the steps, and the back door opened then closed. I hope he's okay.

"He'll be fine."

I spun to find Margaret three feet from me. "I didn't realize I'd spoken aloud."

Her eyes danced with a gentle smile. "You didn't. Your expression told me what you were thinking."

"What happened to his mother?"

She licked her lips, swallowed hard, and took a

deep breath before she answered. "Drunk driver. Jake was twelve."

I closed my eyes, unable to bear the twin-barbed spear of empathy and memory that impaled my heart. "Oh my God."

A soft hand caressed my shoulder. "How old were you?"

"Your aunt isn't the only one who's psychic."

"I'm not. And she isn't my aunt. As far as I know, we aren't related."

I stared. I know it's not polite, but I couldn't seem to pull my gaze from hers. "Huh?"

Margaret chuckled. "Everyone calls her Aunt Octavia. To be honest, I'm not sure who she's related to. She's everybody's aunt, everybody's guardian, and a very sweet lady."

"What she said about Jake and me..."

"Sit down and we'll have a chat."

I climbed onto the second stool at the counter, and Margaret set a hot cup of coffee in front of me. "I should be working," I said.

"Did you lose your mom or dad?"

"Dad." I looked away, and hoped she didn't see the tears filling my eyes.

"How old were you?"

"Five." My voice broke in spite of all my effort to hide the emotion filling my throat. Wispy bits of memory floated in front of me: Daddy smiling when I rode my new bike for the first time, his deep laugh as he swung me around high up in the air, the sound of Mom yelling at him the night before he took off, me standing at the big living room window waiting and waiting and waiting every day for Daddy to come back home, mom scolding me for being so foolish.

He never returned.

"Are you all right?"

What? Oh, Margaret was talking to me. Focus. I quickly wiped at my eyes and forced my lips into a smile. "I'm fine."

"Would you like to talk about it?"

I took a sip of the coffee to get my bearings. "It happened a long time ago."

"It doesn't matter how long ago things happened," she told me. "What matters is how torn up your heart is."

My heart was currently held together with duct tape. "I really need to get those photos done."

She gripped my arm. "When you're ready to talk, I'll be here."

"Thanks, but I'm fine."

"*When* you're ready."

She held my gaze, and I looked into her softly caring eyes. Margaret was the kind of mother I'd always fantasized about. The kind I'd never believed existed. The kind I would have given my favorite doll to have. "Thank you," I whispered.

She smiled and let go with both her hand and her gaze.

I scurried off to take pictures, and wonder what it was about this little town that seemed determined to knock my life a few degrees off north.

*\*\*\*\**

Bits of afternoon sun sprinkled through the leaves at the Ugly Creek State Park. It was here the former students of Ugly Creek High School gathered for the next chapter in the unfolding Ugly Reunion soap opera.

Jake insisted I take off early to attend, and Margaret insisted on driving me.

So there I wandered among picnic tables and trees and people I didn't know. I was uncomfortable at first, but then the warm breeze reached out to touch my hair as it moved to caress leaves and pine needles. At the gentle touch, my shoulders began to release from their frozen position near my ears.

Memories played in my head. Good ones. Picnics and birthday parties at the state park near Crooked Hollow. Trips to the lake. A vacation spent in a cabin in the mountains. Our last night there, my brother Brandon and I sat on the porch and watched the lightning and felt the roar of thunder. We shuddered and laughed and felt totally alive until the rain changed direction and the hard driving drops soaked us before we could reach the cabin door.

I smiled. It had been worth the hour-long screaming reprimand from our stepfather. Brandon and I had laughed about that day for years afterward.

"How did your first day go?"

Maddie's voice jerked me back to the present, and I reluctantly pulled away from the past to answer her. "It went okay."

She nodded, her eyes unreadable behind her large, dark sunglasses. This was her Audrey Hepburn look, and she carried it off with style. She wore black capris, a cute, sky blue, sleeveless shirt, and an adorable pair of strappy sandals. Her long, blonde hair was pulled into a ponytail which cascaded down her back and glistened in the dappled sunlight.

I glanced down at the vintage sundress I'd chosen to wear. I wasn't going for a look, I was simply being me. I sighed internally.

"So you like working there, huh?"

She was fishing, and I didn't want to be the poor trout on her hook. "I enjoyed taking pictures of beautiful antiques."

There was a pause. "So, how is Jake?"

And there was the bait. "I didn't know he'd lost his mother."

Her head jerked slightly, and I could feel the heat of her curiosity through the dark lenses. "He told you about that?"

"No. Actually, Aunt Octavia came by. She had a message from his mother." The memory of the pain in his eyes as he walked away tore at me. "What she said upset him." I swallowed. "Your mom explained that she'd died when he was twelve."

"Oh man, it always upsets him when Aunt Octavia does that." The dark glasses had come off, and Maddie was carefully touching a tissue to the corners of her eyes.

Well, that told me quite a bit. "Has Aunt Octavia ever given you a message from your dad?"

"No. And I hope she never does."

"I'd love to hear from my father." I said it before I thought and looked away to keep Maddie from seeing the tears I felt filling my eyes. Stupid tears. Why should I be crying over a man who obviously hadn't cared about me?

Maddie's hand touched my arm. "Maybe if we talked to her she could help you somehow."

I blinked back the newly threatening tears. "Maybe tell me why he hated us so much?"

"Maybe tell you if he's still alive."

I felt long repressed rage boil slowly over the top. "What if he is? What if he's alive and well and being a great dad to a new family? How would that help anything?"

"I'm sorry. I don't know what to say."

I closed my eyes for a moment, forcing back the hot steam of my anger. "It's okay. It's over, you know? Over and done with. He left me. And Brandon. And Mom. There's nothing I can do about that."

She put a hand on my arm. "If you want to talk, I'm here."

I had to swallow back the emotion before I could say, "Thanks, Maddie."

I gave her a quick hug, and she headed over to join the cheerleaders. I wandered around for a while, watching birds, squirrels, and people. It was a family event, so there were a lot of spouses and children.

I got a kick out of the kids running around. I love kids, maybe because I relate to them better than to most adults. Kids are honest; they tell it like it is. They aren't real impressed by the trappings of wealth and power either. They see people the way they really are. I like that.

I managed to get myself involved in a toddler game of Nerf football, and later was able to hold a really sweet little nine-month old. He was teething and drooled all over the place, but it was worth it when he grinned at me.

Shadows grew longer as the sun dipped behind the mountain and the steamy air began to cool. I wandered around the area, trying to find a place where I felt even vaguely comfortable when I caught a glimpse of Jake toward the edge of the festivities. He sat alone at a table, facing the party, but not taking part. He looked lonely. And tired. And sexy as hell.

Bad Stephie.

I glanced guiltily toward where Maddie laughed and squealed with her cheerleader buddies.

I didn't actually make a decision, somehow I just found myself walking toward the far end of the area. "Hey, Jake."

He smiled warmly. "Thanks for helping with the pictures."

"My pleasure. You have beautiful things to take pictures of."

I tossed a glance back toward Maddie. Hurting my closest friend was not in my game plan for this trip. I was not my mother; I would not put a man ahead of the people I loved.

"Let's take a walk."

I nodded and together we headed toward the thick copse of trees closest to the picnic area. We'd only gone a little way when I felt Jake's warm hand against my lower back. The touch sent all manner of tingles up and down my spine and to more interesting places too. He edged me into a deep shadow next to an ancient oak, then moved in to face me. He looked deep into my eyes. The fingers of one hand gently, reverently touched my cheek.

"I don't want to make things more complicated for you," he said. "But you're like whipped cream on a sundae, and I want to take a big bite."

I swallowed hard and tried to convince my hormone-charged body that being loyal to a friend was much more important than any sparks flying between me and this man. Sadly those sparks had shorted a couple of my circuits and instead of heading back where I should be, I put my hand over his and pressed his fingers more firmly against my face.

"Oh, Stephie." The words were followed by a groan. He pulled me close as I stretched up to him.

His mouth moved over mine and our lips fused with desire. His hands slid down my back leaving scorched skin behind.

I pulled him closer, my fingers sliding under his polo shirt to explore his back as if he had the secrets of the universe written in Braille on his skin.

One of his hands moved to the front and managed to find its way into the neckline of my dress. His fingers moved over the top of my breast, and I felt like I'd been turned into a rocket and aimed for the moon. I heard a long moan I only vaguely realized had come from me.

He kissed his way from my mouth across my cheek to my ear. "I don't even know your real name," he whispered.

"Buffy," I heard myself saying. "Buffy Stephanova."

"Doesn't suit you."

"I agree."

And then his lips took possession of mine again, and I was floating in space looking down at a fiery volcano. And I wanted it. Bad.

He pulled away, and I bit my lip to keep from crying out.

"I'm sure as hell not going to do this on the ground fifty feet from my entire class and their families." He took my hand in his. "Even if you do make me crazy."

I trembled and my body was on fire, but even in the state I was in I realized he was right. "You're a gentleman," I managed.

He chuckled. "Gentleman, huh?"

"Yes."

He brushed a stray strand of hair off my face. "I'll see you at the store tomorrow." And he was gone.

I stood there for a few minutes getting my breathing under control and my focus back to the same zip code as me. Still, my heart was racing and my face was hot when I started toward the rest of the group. I hung back to give myself time to calm down and hopefully Maddie wouldn't realize immediately I'd thrown her over for a big bad bag of sexy.

"Hello, *Buffy*," Butch said, as he stepped out from behind one of the huge oaks. "So you and Blackwood have a thing. Figures. Big man quarterback has to have everything in a skirt that walks past him. What would he think if he knew who you really are?"

This was getting old. Fast. "Look, I don't know what you think you know about me, but you need to find a new hobby."

A slow, nasty grin split his face. "I read you went to a big college. What I wonder is how you managed to pay for that fancy education. Maybe you'd like to demonstrate." He reached for his zipper.

My hand popped his face, leaving a bright red handprint behind. "Son of a monkey's ass."

I turned and hurried away before I decided to tear out his ugly heart. Men. All they were good for was messing up a girl's life. Damn 'em all to hell. I sure didn't need one. I was just fine by myself, thank you very much.

I walked aimlessly for a while, staying close to the populated area, but far enough away I had a bit of privacy. As I worked at getting my anger back under control, I tried hard not to remember how my mother and stepfather had held the strings on every single penny I used to go to Columbia. I'd wanted to get a job, but I also wanted to take a heavy course load so I could get through and be free to live my own life. So I put up with it all, including the yelling and hitting from a stepfather I loathed. A man I'd left my little brother to face alone.

I found the rectangular green building that held the public bathroom, and splashed water on my face. There were no paper towels, so I air-dried.

I started back toward the picnic area determined I was going to find Madison and stay beside her for the rest of this reunion-festival thing. She was my friend, and I loved her. I would not allow a man to make me lose sight of that goal. I was not my mother!

I was walking back when I heard Butch's voice. "I don't like being blamed for something I didn't do."

"We all know you did it, dude. Why don't you be a man and admit it."

"It was him," Butch's voice said. "Quit blaming me."

I edged closer, careful to keep a tree between me and Butch's line of sight.

"I also do not like being blamed for what I did not do."

The voice was coarse and sounded very much as if the person speaking was not a native English speaker. German maybe? I edged a bit closer to try to get a glimpse without being spotted.

"Why don't you just own up, Johnson and leave the big guy alone?"

The father of one of the junior pageant contestants stomped out from behind the copse of trees, and I ducked backward to keep him from seeing me.

"I was always careful," Butch was saying. "I always put the butt out. I know it wasn't me, and I saw you that night."

I edged closer to eavesdrop...I mean investigate the situation.

"I was there," the gravelly voice said. "But I was not smoking."

"You had a cigarette in your hand."

"You are mistaken."

"Damn it! I know it was you. I don't care who you are, you don't get to use me as your scapegoat."

Butch turned and stomped off. I watched him go, until a sound had me looking back toward where the confrontation had taken place. There was movement, and then I saw him. Huge, furry. It was just a glimpse, but I was sure.

"They do exist," I whispered.

And then the significance of what I'd just heard hit me. There was more to this little town than I'd ever imagined, and my curiosity was screaming at me to find out more.

I was beginning to be truly fascinated by odd, little Ugly Creek, Tennessee.

Chapter 10

I figured the drive to work the next morning was the perfect opportunity to get a few answers. We'd barely gotten out of the driveway when I decided to put my theory to the test. "Margaret, what caused the fire?"

She didn't answer for a time, but I saw how her shoulders had tensed, how her knuckles had gone white where she gripped the steering wheel.

"The best the investigators could figure was it started behind the boys' locker room. The theory is that somebody was smoking back there."

"Do they know who?"

I saw her swallow. "There wasn't really enough left to figure it out."

I touched her arm. "I'm sorry; I know it has to be hard to talk about."

She flashed me a weak smile. "It's gotten easier over the years."

"Does it make you angry, that nobody was ever charged?"

"Oh heavens, no. It was an accident. Some kid was smoking. Somehow he dropped a lit cigarette, probably didn't even realize he'd done it. Until later."

She cleared her throat and shifted until she sat straighter. "Besides, whoever it was has to live with the guilt. I believe that would be the worst possible punishment."

"You're right. That would be awful."

I looked out the window. I knew something about that living with guilt thing. I unzipped my purse and pulled the picture out of my wallet. The photo of a ten-year-old boy. A shot I'd taken years ago with my brand new Minolta thirty-five millimeter single lens reflex. I bought the camera with my fifteenth-birthday money, and was chewed out royally for not spending the money on something "practical." I still couldn't figure out what was more practical than a camera.

"Did you take that picture?"

I jumped before I could stop myself.

Margaret patted my arm. "I'm sorry, honey. I didn't mean to startle you."

"I was lost in thought."

"He's a nice looking young man."

"That's my brother Brandon. He's five years younger than me, and was just admitted to graduate school. Wait a minute, how did you know I took that shot?"

She chuckled. "It's your style. Candid, but artistic. Catching the essence of your subject."

I thought about it for a moment. "Maddie's been showing you my work, hasn't she?"

"Yes, but I also read *Capitol Spy* every month."

I leaned back in my seat, running a finger over the photo in my hand. "My work for the *Spy* isn't all that artistic."

"You don't give yourself enough credit. What you do for them may not be the sort of thing you think of as artistic, but your talent is infused into every photograph you take. Trust me, Stephie. You have a wonderful style."

She pulled into the parking lot behind Blackwood Antiques, and I grabbed my camera bag and laptop.

Dingo met us and I dropped to my heels to give the dog his belly scratch. I knew when Jake stooped beside me because the air started sparking between us.

"You're spoiling my dog," Jake's deep voice vibrated through me, strumming my nerves like a violin.

"He deserves to be spoiled," I told him.

"Oh, you think so, do you?"

I smiled at the huge ball of soft fur sprawled in the floor in front of me. "Look at him, he's gorgeous and sweet and friendly. What more could you want in a dog?"

Jake's hand suddenly closed over mine. The touch of his rough, warm hand had me gasping for breath, and trying hard not to let him know how much he affected me. "You had a dog once, didn't you?"

"Yes."

"When you were a kid growing up in Alabama?"

Everything stopped. Everything. The world, my heart, my brain, my hands, my life, my lungs. Little black dots began to pop onto the edges of my vision.

"Stephie?"

I gasped in a fresh breath of oxygen, clearing my vision and starting my heart again. My brain, though, was still muddled. "How long have you known?"

He shrugged. "I'd suspected for a while."

"Really?"

He chuckled. "Sweetheart, your accent pops out now and again."

"My *what*? Do you know how hard I've worked to get rid of my accent? Most people don't hear it. How can you?"

He rolled off his heels into a sitting position and leaned back on his hands. "There's nothing wrong with having a Southern accent, you know."

"I don't want one."

"Why not?"

I played with Dingo's fur while I got my panic a little more under control. "I hate where I grew up."

He was watching me; I could see him out of the corner of my eye. "What did Crooked Tree Hollow do to you?"

"How did you find out?"

"My best friend's a computer geek. You think I can't use the Internet?"

My breath caught as I stiffened, prompting Dingo to scramble to his feet. "I just didn't like it there. Okay?"

"Your family has lived there for years, right?"

"Generations."

Dingo decided being scratched was worth the risk of being startled again and flopped back down.

"I saw one article that said your father was the mayor for eight years?"

"Stepfather," I spoke with my teeth clenched together to prevent the vile words I seriously wanted to say. I tried to get up, but Jake had his hand firmly around my wrist.

"Not a nice man, I take it."

"Just because he goes to church every Sunday and he was the fricking mayor, doesn't make him a saint." I stopped, closed my eyes and wondered what in the world had possessed me to say something so transparent.

Jake tugged me against the warm, solid wall of his chest. "What did he do to you?"

Seriously unwelcome tears flooded my eyes and I fought hard to hold them back. "He just isn't a nice man."

"He hurt you."

"Not only me." He'd hurt Brandon too, and I'd left my little brother there to take the heat.

"He hit you?"

I pulled away. "I don't want to talk about my stepfather, okay? He wasn't exactly nice to me, but it's over I'm getting on with my life. So, I'd appreciate it if you'd just forget the whole thing."

"If that's what you want."

"It is."

"I'm here if you change your mind."

I met his gaze then, trying to convey the almost overwhelming gratefulness that welled up inside me. Odd. Here in this small town I kept running into supportive, caring people. How very different than the place I'd grown up.

I shoved those syrupy feelings back into the most cobwebbed corner of my mind and gave Dingo a final head scratch. "I'm going to get freshened up."

"Take your time."

I nodded my thanks and shut myself in the closet-sized bathroom off the back room. I looked into the mirror over the sink, and saw the wide, scared eyes of the child I thought I'd left behind. No wonder Jake had been so sweet to me. It wasn't the caring of a man for a woman he was attracted to; instead it had been the caring of an adult for a pathetic child.

I splashed water on my face, forced the pieces of

myself back together, fixed my makeup, took a deep breath, and headed into the store. I had a job to do and I'd be damned if a bastard like the man my traitorous mother had married would keep me from doing it.

There were customers when I got to the front, and both Jake and Margaret were busy. I got right to work by setting up my equipment and pulling the shots up into the appropriate software on my laptop.

They left me alone, and by eleven I was finished with the first set of photos.

"Wow! Those are amazing shots."

I smiled at Jake, who stood behind me looking at the computer screen. "Thank you."

He pointed at a photo of a roll top desk I'd converted to gray tones and then used a yellowish-red tint to make it look like an antique photo. "I'd have never thought of that, but it makes a lot of sense."

"I'm trying several different techniques; you can pick what you want to use." I grinned. "No extra charge."

An artery in his neck jumped and his eyes went abruptly dark. I swallowed hard. Maybe he did see me as a desirable woman after all.

"I'm going to lunch; call my cell if you get overwhelmed." With that, Margaret walked out the door.

"I've, um, got some inventory I need to take care of," Jake said.

I nodded, but he'd already turned to go. Even with my eyes glued to the screen, I could tell exactly where he was. Like heat-seeking missiles, my senses zeroed in on him.

"Maddie hates his guts," I muttered to myself. But

she really didn't. I knew that. I wasn't quite sure what my friend felt for Jake, but hatred wasn't it.

I was focused on trying new ways to present the merchandise when I heard the bell over the door tinkle. I glanced up as a woman walked in. Designer jeans, four-inch heels, sleeveless blouse that looked suspiciously like silk, something about her seemed to yell, "Money." Her jutting chin and perfect posture said she planned to get what she wanted without spending much of said money.

I looked around, but Jake was nowhere in sight.

The newcomer was looking at a beautiful hand-carved table, and beginning to glance around.

I was considering running to the back to find him when her gaze caught mine. So instead, I walked over to her. "May I help you?"

"The tag says forty-five hundred for this little table. That seems rather high."

The customer's expression was one I'd seen many times in D.C., Sly. Calculating. The woman knew the table was worth much more.

Thankfully, I remembered a few facts from Jake's tour yesterday. "This table is nineteenth century mahogany with a marble top. It's a beautiful piece, well worth what Mr. Blackwood is asking for it. Personally, I'd have asked a great deal more."

The woman raised one eyebrow. "Well, it's fortuitous you aren't the one setting the prices."

I smiled innocently. "Yes, I suppose so."

The woman touched a well-manicured finger over a tiny chip in the marble top. "It has a number of damaged spots."

"Three."

The customer blinked. "I beg your pardon?"

"The table has two tiny chips in the marble and one, all but invisible, spot at the top of one leg. Not bad for more than a century of use, don't you think?"

"I'll pay three thousand for it."

Ah, the game was on. I pretended to consider for a moment, then looked her directly in the eye. "I'd have to clear it with the owner, but I might be able to get you forty-three hundred."

"That's insulting!"

I saw the desire in the woman's eyes. I had her on the hook. "It's an excellent deal, and you know it."

"I could go somewhere else."

*Please don't let me lose this sale!* "Well, you certainly can, if you believe you can find a piece of this quality at a lower price."

The woman made as if she was going to walk out the door, but just before she got there she turned. "Thirty-eight hundred."

"Four even—and I'll have to clear it with the owner."

"Fine."

"Wait here and I'll go get him."

I'd barely gotten to the counter when Jake suddenly appeared.

"I told the lady I might be able to convince you to go four thousand for the marble top table. I know that's a big discount." I shot him a glance I hoped conveyed the fear playing dodgeball with my insides.

"Hmm, well, that's a really nice piece. I hate to go that low." He walked over to study the table, pulling at his bottom lip with a thumb and forefinger. "I suppose I might be able to let it go for four."

The woman pulled out a checkbook and began writing. "I'll have it picked up first thing in the morning."

"That'll be fine," Jake said, as he took the check.

The woman went out the door, and I let out a long, wonderful sigh of relief as I collapsed against the counter. "You did that on purpose."

His wide-eyed innocent expression would have been amusing at another time. "Did what on purpose?"

"Threw me to the sharks... I mean the customers. Alone! And I don't work for you."

"Yes, you do."

Still with the innocent expression. That irritating, pain in the tail, hunk o' man. "Not as a salesperson."

He grinned. "That's too bad, because you're a good one."

I was still irritated with him, but the compliment was nice. "You think so?"

"Yes, Buffy, I do."

Before I even thought, I smacked him playfully on the arm. "Don't call me that."

"Hey! Do you always hit your bosses?"

"Only when they call me *that* name."

He was inches from me. I longed to touch his face. I longed to kiss his lips. I longed to consider what a future with him would be like.

What the hell was wrong with me?

Thankfully, Margaret came back before I threw myself at him—or proposed marriage.

"Stephie made a sale while you were gone." There was pride in Jake's voice.

Margaret's face lit up. "Congratulations! Make sure he gives you your commission."

I narrowed my eyes at him. "Commission? You didn't say anything about a commission."

"How about we discuss it over lunch?"

"Make him buy," Margaret said.

Jake held up his hands in surrender. "I was planning on it. Hold the fort down, Margaret."

"Don't I always?"

"Yes, you do. You're a valuable employee, Mrs. Clark."

She didn't even bat an eyelash. "So when do I get my raise?"

Jake blinked. Then a tiny smile pulled at his lips for just a second. "Sorry, Margaret, I can't afford to increase your salary right now. I just took on a second employee."

"Fine, so I should expect my raise how soon after Stephie leaves for D.C.?"

Jake stopped in his tracks, head down. Stephie saw a smile on his lips, but when he glanced over his shoulder at Margaret, it was with a straight face. "I'll have to get back to you on that."

"You do that, Blackwood."

Jake took my arm and all but pulled me toward the back. He stopped once we were out of earshot of Margaret. "If we go to a restaurant, we're both going to be uncomfortable. If you're willing to go upstairs to my apartment, you, Dingo, and I can have a nice, quiet, private lunch."

The idea excited me a little more than I would like. "Your apartment, huh?"

"Yes, my apartment. It's private. And if you're worried, Dingo will be there as chaperone.

"Well, I do trust Dingo."

I followed a chuckling Jake up the stairs and through a door that looked as if it could have been put up when the store was built. His place was basic, functional. Green, comfy looking couch. Matching chair. Flat screen television mounted on the wall behind a gorgeous, hand-tooled table. I didn't know enough to be able to date the piece, but I was quite sure it was old and probably valuable. There was a fantastic chair in the corner. Also antique. Nothing really went together; there was no theme to the room. It was quite obvious no highly paid decorator had worked on the place. Simply beautiful pieces placed so the occupants could enjoy them.

It was my dream apartment.

Dingo barreled toward me, all but knocking me over. I gave the furry ball of happiness the requested head scratch.

"What do you think?"

I looked into Jake's proudly shining eyes. "I love what you've done with the place."

He chuckled. "Glad you like it."

"So it's true, you really can't bring yourself to let go of some pieces."

"Like I told you earlier, I have to watch myself, or I'd be broke and this place would be a storage facility."

"I admire your self-control."

A slow, sexy smile wandered across Jake's face. "Thank you."

Though I stood a couple of feet from him, I could feel the heat coming from his body. Strong, warm, welcome heat. I breathed in spicy aftershave and pure Jake. My lungs said move closer. My heart danced in pure joy.

"Do you like meatball subs?" he asked.

What? Oh, lunch. "I love meatball subs." I do, don't I?

He smiled and turned toward the cute little kitchen. I followed and plopped down at the small table. The counters and appliances were white. The walls were reddish orange. The kitchen was clean with dishes washed and neatly stacked in the wooden drainer. Curtains with bright yellow flowers decorated the windows.

I felt my forehead tighten into a frown. Either Jake had accessed his feminine side when he decorated the place, or a woman had been involved somehow. Ether scenario could explain a few things. As much as I didn't want to, I had to know.

"My sister helped me decorate."

*Sister. Yes!* I smiled up at him. "Are you sure you aren't related to Aunt Octavia? I'm pretty sure you're psychic too."

Jake touched his fingers to his head, and closed his eyes. "I'm having a premonition."

"Oh really?"

"Yep." He turned, took a plate in his hand and set it in front of me. "I predict that this is the best meatball sub you've ever tasted."

Twenty minutes later, I decided not only was Jake psychic, he was also an amazing cook. His creation truly was the best meatball sub, it might even be the best *anything* I'd ever eaten.

He'd made four sandwiches—one for me, two for himself, and one for Dingo. I was leaning back in my chair, Dingo was sprawled in the floor, half under the table, and Jake was looking at me like I was dessert.

Umm, that thought stirred interesting places in my body.

He stood to pick up the empty dish in front of me; our gazes locked. Then he leaned toward me, and my breath sucked in and caught. Closer, closer. His lips touched mine and a fiery comet streaked from the sky to the point of lip contact and through my body, lighting fires as it went.

Jake put the plate down and pulled me up into his arms. I stood centimeters from him, and breathed in the spicy male scent of him. Odd, maybe, but I found myself thinking how he was definitely not the soft, middle-aged dude central casting would send for an antiques dealer. He was more like a sculpted piece of granite. A warm, sexy piece.

He pulled me tight against him and I discovered *all* of him was hard. Oh my.

The kisses got deeper, and my heart banged harder against my ribs. Jake held me close as his hands roamed over my back, hips, sides, breasts.

Through the hormone fog, I vaguely realized my arms were around Jake's neck, I pulled him closer, rubbing against him like a cat. Good grief, I was throwing myself at him like a lovesick teenager.

He looked into my eyes, and I held his gaze. We communicated without a word. We both knew we should stop. Now. This wasn't right. Things were too complicated. We shouldn't. *I* shouldn't.

And we both knew we would.

I'm not really sure how we wound up in the bedroom; we just seemed to suddenly be there. Clothes flew and we fell onto the big bed. Jake's hands were everywhere and his lips were close behind. My body tingled and vibrated. He touched, he licked, he made me feel like I was the only thing in his world.

He spent the better part of the next hour proving he knew how to make a woman very, very happy.

I was dozing against his strong chest when I realized he was staring at me. "Is something wrong?"

He smiled and ran a finger down my cheek. "Not a thing. But I need to get back down to the store."

Reality dropped on me like a bucket of cold water and I sucked in a hard breath. "I'm supposed to be working."

Jake chuckled. "I'll have a word with your boss."

"Very funny." I felt my face heating and to distract myself, I did what I'd wanted to do since I met this enigmatic man. I ran a finger gently over the scar on his cheek, following the flat paleness to the earlobe that was also scarred. "Throwing myself at my boss wasn't very professional of me."

"You didn't." He kissed my nose. "I hope you don't sue me for sexual harassment."

I lay back and smiled into dark, erotic eyes. "I had too much fun for that, big boy."

"You stay right where you are for a bit. I'll go on down and tell Margaret you and Dingo are bonding over a dog bone."

He was covering, for both of us. "Thank you."

He shrugged. "It's a small town. I don't want to start people talking."

"Wouldn't be a good thing."

"Nope." He kissed me, and the stoked fire flared again. He pulled away and stood, naked and gorgeous. "I'd better get going while I still can."

As he turned toward the bathroom, I saw evidence

he was feeling the fire again himself. The shower started, and I thought briefly of joining him there.

No, no, no. Jake was right. We needed to get back to work. I knew from hard experience how small towns could be. My mind went on a journey back in time, to another small town. High school was bad enough without hearing almost daily how wonderful your stepfather was, and how I should be so very grateful to have him looking out for me.

Then there was the time I actually listened to the propaganda about confidential help being there if you needed it. I talked to a guidance counselor about my stepdad. I didn't tell her everything, just that he yelled a lot. That night, I got the worst beating of my life. The bitch had called him, told him I was trying to cause trouble.

Apparently it wasn't just my stepdad the guidance counselor told, because the rumors after that were frequently about how I was a spoiled, ungrateful, little ass. Your small town tax dollars at work.

My little trip down Wish I Could Forget Lane had the effect of an icy shower. By the time Jake came out of the bathroom, wrapped only in a towel, I wanted nothing more than to get myself cleaned up, go downstairs, and pretend nothing happened.

Jake dressed, kissed me lightly, and headed for the door. "See you in a few."

He headed out, and I forced myself to slide from the warmth of his bed.

I took a careful shower, protecting my hair and as much of my makeup as I could. I dressed, snuck down the stairs, grabbed my purse and slipped into the shop bathroom to freshen my makeup.

Then I went out to the floor and pretended to be totally occupied with the pictures and my laptop.

Before long, I felt someone watching me. I glanced up to see Margaret smiling knowingly in my direction. My face blazed as I turned back to my computer. I tried to pretend I was wholly immersed in my work while in reality I fought the urge to run out the back door.

She knew. Maybe it was the smile I couldn't completely wipe off my face. Maybe it was my damp hair. Maybe she'd heard something from upstairs. Whatever the reason, I knew she knew, and I did the thing folks have done since the Neanderthals walked the earth: I wondered if I could, in fact, die of embarrassment.

Jake came in the front door and handed Margaret a small white bag, then he came toward me, and held out a second one. "Cookies from the bakery down the street. They're wonderful."

I reached in and took one, seeing my hand shake as I did.

"I got Margaret a prune scone. She loves the things."

The smell of the cookie in my hand had a calming effect on me. "Bribery?"

He shrugged. "I prefer to think of it as a reward for being a loyal employee. She knows how to keep her mouth shut. She used to work for lawyers, after all."

I peeked around Jake to see Margaret thumbing through a magazine. She took a bite of her pastry as an expression of contentment crossed her face, then went back to the magazine.

"Would you like a Coke?"

"I'd love one."

He took off and I sniffed the cookie again. My mouth was too dry to eat it, but just the scent was enough to brighten my day.

Jake brought me the drink, and I took a sip. When my mouth didn't resemble the Mojave Desert anymore, I allowed myself to savor the cookie. He brought me another one, and I decided we'd expended enough calories earlier to cover two little cookies. Okay, not so little cookies, but not so few calories either.

Eventually the cookies worked their magic, and I was able to focus on my work. The gorgeous subject matter helped, and before long I was happily playing with various effects and cropping the pictures in different places.

"You're a fantastic artist."

I looked up into Jake's dark, warm eyes. "Thank you."

"The stuff you do for *Capitol Spy* is good, but it doesn't show your real talent."

My breath caught behind the top of my breastbone and expanded, making my chest ache. "You've seen my work for *Spy*?"

He beamed me a wide, sexy grin that had my toenails sweating. "You don't think I'd hire a photographer without seeing her work first, do you?"

How nice, he'd seen my work. He thought I was good.

Wait a minute. Just *when* had he seen my work? I opened my mouth to ask, but he'd already turned and had headed over to talk to Margaret. I sure as Hades wasn't going anywhere near her right now. I could wait.

But I'd find out. Jake couldn't hide info from me. I work for a publication that prides itself on finding out secrets, after all. I knew a few tricks.

I smiled evilly. Just you wait, Blackwood.

The rest of the afternoon moved along pretty fast. There was a steady stream of customers, mostly tourists, possibly in town for the Big Foot Festival. Which was one more thing I needed to use my awesome snooping ability on. I'd seen one of the big hairy varmints. I longed to get a shot of one. To prove they existed—maybe to myself. The idea blew across my mind like an out of control rocket: one clear photo of Bigfoot and my career would be made.

An arrow of guilt immediately impaled my heart with such impact I gasped and all but collapsed over my laptop. The repercussions to the creatures—and to the town—would likely be devastating. Oh well, I didn't have a picture, so I could safely worry about that tomorrow. Or the day after. Hey, if it was good enough for Scarlett O'Hara it's good enough for me.

A little more than two hours after I'd dodged that inner turmoil, it was time to go back to Margaret's house. With Margaret. Just the two of us. Alone in her car. Oh boy.

I smiled at her, climbed into the Mustang, and opened my laptop so I could pretend I was doing something important.

"You don't need to be embarrassed, hon. I grew up in the Sixties. You know, the age of free love."

It was like one of those nightmares where you show up for a presentation at work, only to find you're buck naked. I stared at the computer screen, and tried to pretend this conversation wasn't happening, but the dang thing was going dark. It was a new battery. Why hadn't it charged?

"Breathe."

Huh?

I felt Margaret put her hand on my arm. "Breathe, Stephie, or you're gonna pass out."

I nodded, and took a couple of slow, deep breaths. She was right, I did feel less lightheaded.

"That's a very attractive couple. Friends of yours?"

I looked at my laptop, and was horrified to see I'd inadvertently opened it to one of the couples I'd photographed. "Acquaintances." I shrugged and hoped to downplay the whole thing. "I enjoy taking shots of couples. It's kind of a hobby of mine."

She nodded. "Sounds like a fun thing to do."

"It is. I see so much bad stuff; it's great to relax a little. I like printing out the shots and giving them to the couples."

"That's really sweet of you, Stephie."

"I get more out of it than they do."

I leaned back and looked at the woman behind the wheel. All my embarrassment melted away, replaced by a strong desire to get to know her better. "So you and Maddie discuss journalism?" My own mother couldn't care less about photography or my job.

Margaret shrugged. "It's something we have in common."

"In common? But didn't you work for a law firm before you started working for Jake."

"Well, that's true, but I was a journalism major in college. I worked as a reporter until I had Madison and started looking for a job with more regular hours. Once I started with the firm, I found I truly enjoyed the work."

Doing what you enjoy. That's the way to live your

life. In theory, anyway.

She told me some stories of her exploits as a reporter for a Nashville newspaper. By the time we pulled into Margaret's driveway, I had developed a great respect for the woman.

"Thank you, Margaret," I told her as we walked toward the house.

"For what, hon?"

"For giving me a ride, and for sharing some of your life." And for keeping your mouth shut.

Margaret gave me a quick sideways hug. "I'm happy to be of help."

As I trucked up the stairs, I realized there was an extra car in the driveway. A silver Lexus. Maybe I should have paid more attention because I opened the bedroom door and walked in on Maddie and Liza having a primp party.

Clothes covered both beds. Makeup was strewed over Maddie's dresser, chest, and the desk she'd probably used to do homework when she was in high school.

"Hi, Stephie." Maddie spoke without moving her head. Probably because Liza was diligently rolling Maddie's long, golden hair on hot rollers. I'd have thought the cast on her arm would slow her down, but the hair-rolling was moving right along. "We're getting ready for the pageant tonight," Maddie said.

I managed to keep the groan mostly inward. We've already established beauty pageants aren't one of My Favorite Things. And this was the big girl version. No cute little darlings for me to go nuts about.

"Oh get over it, Steph. You're a girl, you should like pageants. They're a lot of fun, you know."

Oh boy. I heard the irritation in her voice. Maddie was still pissed I had kissed Jake and was now working for him. If she knew what else we'd been doing…

I wasn't about to allow myself to think of that. The way things were going, either Maddie or Liza could probably read my mind.

I started to tell her I was finished with the project I was doing for Blackwood Antiques, then rethought the situation. Probably better I didn't bring up the subject at all.

So I gave into the inevitable. "Okay, so what does one wear to a Miss Ugly Creek Pageant?"

"Well, for most people it doesn't really matter." Maddie gave me a sideways glance. She might as well have delivered it while looking down her nose, for all the dismissal in her voice.

"But for former winners like Liza—junior year— and myself—senior year—it's a very big deal."

My fists tightened, even as tears filled my heart. "Congratulations," I managed.

I went to the closet where my clothes were hung, grabbed an emerald sleeveless blouse and a black pencil skirt. I jerked a bra and panties out of my assigned drawer. "I need a shower," I said as I went out, not caring much whether either of them heard me or not.

As the hot water sprayed over me, I allowed the tears I'd been holding back to fall. I understood Maddie was angry with me for consorting with a man she considered the enemy. I also knew she was still angry with her mother for the same offense.

Still, even if I did understand, her attitude had torn into me like a vulture into carrion.

I finished showering, blew my hair dry, put on a bit

of makeup, dressed, and headed down the stairs. The last thing I wanted was another run-in with Miss Junior Year and Miss Senior Year.

Margaret looked up from the pot she was stirring and smiled my way. "You look beautiful, Stephie. That shade of green really makes those gorgeous eyes of yours shine."

"Thank you," I said, wondering if it was the tears I was holding back as hard as I could that was making my eyes shine.

"Are you all right?" She put a hand on my shoulder.

"I'm just not crazy about beauty pageants." Which is true. Not the whole truth, but true nonetheless.

"I don't really like them either. Maddie loves them though."

I felt Margaret's hand tighten on my shoulder. "Try to remember she's in pain. You can't lock your feelings up in a little box and expect them to stay there. I was hoping she'd use coming home as an opportunity to try to put things right, but that girl is as stubborn as her father was."

Margaret was even more emotionally torn in the battle between Maddie and Jake than I was, and I felt serious sympathy for her. "I do understand, Margaret. I know she's hurting and I want her to be happy. I should have stayed away from Jake Blackwood. She's my friend, and that's more important than a man."

Margaret looked at me, a deep sadness in her eyes. "Sweetie, your loyalty to my daughter is admirable, but please think twice before you destroy any chances you and Jake have, based solely on Maddie's confused feelings about him. I'd hate for you to live with regret

142

long after Jake and Maddie have put aside their differences."

"I think I need some fresh air," I said, as I grabbed my camera and headed out the back door.

Even the screen of the porch made me feel claustrophobic, so I sat on the outside steps. I made a big deal out of cleaning my camera and changing the batteries in case someone was watching—or psychic. But my mind wasn't on photography.

I berated myself as I put my Nikon digital back together. Madison was my closest friend. We're great roommates, work well together, and she truly accepts me, the real me. Not the model of perfection my mother expected, or the stereotype many people seemed to think described everyone from Alabama.

Take that idiot Butch for instance, assuming I'd come from a trailer park. How biased was that? Like everybody in Alabama is poor. Or illiterate. Or redneck.

I grew up in a big house in an expensive neighborhood and attended the best schools in the state. After high school I headed to Columbia University to study journalism, and nailed a job in Washington, D.C., the center of government. Where the action was.

I sighed. At least that's what I'd imagined. Most of the time I was chasing down a lead that never panned out, or managing to catch a legislator or judge or celebrity overindulging in a bar or restaurant. Or if they were female, I'd try to catch them without makeup, if male, with makeup. Whoop-dee-do. What do I care? Why anyone cares is beyond me.

Shaking the evil thoughts away, I focused on the things I had to be thankful for, like Maddie, the bestest roommate in the history of the world. And my job. It paid the bills quite well, thank you. Even in the expensive city of Washington, D.C.

Or at least that's what I told myself every morning as I got dressed for work.

Movement caught my attention, and I looked out into the wooded area behind Margaret's house. In the afternoon sun I could clearly see her backyard butted up against the mountains. A cool breeze stirred the leaves and cooled the hot Southern summer heat a bit. That's probably what I'd seen, the leaves moving.

I took a long, deep breath of fresh air, and felt relaxation pull at my muscles. For a moment I considered telling Maddie and Liza I was too tired to go to the pageant. I could curl up on the porch and read that Janet Evanovich novel I bought almost a month ago, but hadn't even had time to open.

*No!* I was here to support Maddie. Just because she had Liza to do that, and she was pissed at me anyway, was no excuse. I'd made a commitment and I intended to follow through.

This time the movement was big and the foliage rustled. No doubt something large was in a bush behind one of the oak trees. My first instinct was to raise my camera; I was a champion catch-a-celebrity-at-an-inopportune-moment photojournalist after all. And when I saw what came out from behind the bush my finger triggered the shutter without my even thinking about it.

As I watched the creature turn and run toward the heavier foliage closer to the incline of the mountain, I caught a few more shots. I knew without looking that none were as good as the first, but it was second nature for me to take more.

And then it was gone, and I lowered the Nikon back into my lap. Damn! Ugly Creek was awesome.

The door opened, and I instinctually clicked off the camera. I turned to see Liza's head sticking out the door. "Are you about ready to head out?"

"Whenever you are."

"Give us ten minutes." She started to close the door, but stopped in mid-movement. "I'm really sorry Maddie's being so bitchy. You don't deserve that." I saw her swallow. "Neither does Jake, for that matter."

"What happened between—"I heard Maddie's voice coming our way and bit back the words.

"We'll talk later," Liza whispered, and hurried inside.

I took one more look out into the trees, but saw nothing moving. Sighing, I pulled my tired, frustrated body to its feet. One ugly part of my brain whispered that a picture of a real Bigfoot could make a photojournalist's career.

Or bring that career to an abrupt, painful end.

Chapter 11

The Ugly Creek High School auditorium was done up in a "Reach for the Stars" motif. "Because that's not cliché," I muttered.

"At least they didn't do 'Under the Sea.' Again."

The voice had icy guilt growing in the pit of my stomach, while hot flames of desire fired in points farther south. I turned and looked into warm brown eyes that kicked my pulse up a few notches. "Jake."

He smiled, and guilt fought hard to hold its grip on my conscience. "Stephie."

"I didn't peg you as someone who'd be interested in beauty pageants." I was glad to hear an edge to my voice. He was a chauvinist pig. That explained things. He saw women as meat, as objects, not as real people.

"Just doing my part for Ugly Creek. Blackwood Antiques is one of the pageant sponsors. Actually, pretty much every business in Ugly Creek is."

"Oh." Well, rats.

He took my hand in his and pulled me into the shadows. His lips touched mine and I melted into him, savoring his warm scent, the feel of his body pressed against mine. It felt good, it felt perfect.

But Madison Clark was my closest friend, my roommate, the sister I'd never had.

I pulled back. "This isn't right."

"Because of Madison."

"I came to Ugly Creek to support Maddie; this pageant is important to her."

He took my hand in his and tugged me toward him. "I've never met anyone like you. You mean a lot to me."

"We've only known each other a few days."

"I know it sounds crazy, but I care about you and I want to see where this relationship leads." He pulled me closer to him, his eyes filled with emotion. "Please don't walk out on me just because Maddie did. I don't want to lose you too."

"Jake, don't." I was horrified to hear the hurt in my voice.

He looked toward the floor for a moment, and when he met my gaze again there were tears in his eyes. "Just promise me you'll think about what I said."

He could be acting. He could be leading me on just to get me back in bed, or to get even with Maddie somehow.

But I knew he wasn't. "I promise to think about it."

He touched his lips to mine, kissing me with an intensity I felt into my toes. When he finished, he held me hostage with his gaze for an eternity that wasn't nearly long enough. Then he turned and walked away.

My breath sucked in with a big whoosh of air. I grabbed a wall and leaned over at the waist for a minute to get myself together. I was here for Maddie, my good friend, who'd been there for me many times. Not to mention I had a job I'd agreed to for the local newspaper, and I should get my butt in gear and do it.

I had already decided to make a visual chronology of the event, so I spent the next few minutes rushing from the dressing room to the stage area, to the classroom that once again was converted into a second dressing area, and back to the stage. I documented the frenzy of preparation. Makeup, nerves, dresses, panic, shoes, and sheer exhaustion, I tried to capture it all. When one contestant broke down in frustrated tears, I quietly captured the event and then slipped away feeling like a voyeur.

Then there was the intrigue. The disappearing earrings, the foot planted firmly on an opponent's long skirt, the glances one contestant kept giving another, glances filled with jealousy.

In spite of being witness to underhanded tactics, I was shocked to discover the night wasn't as bad as I'd thought it would be. Except, of course, for that irritating man I couldn't seem to stay away from. Every time I turned a corner, there he was. I could almost believe he was stalking me, except he seemed as surprised to see me as I him. It was more like some sort of perverse force that kept drawing us together. It took some serious effort to keep my mind on my job.

The opening ceremonies were over and the talent portion was well underway when I heard the sound of Butch Johnson's voice. "Well, what do we have here? The famous photographer is slumming. Again."

I took a deep breath and counted to twenty before I turned around. "What do you want?"

Butch's lips pulled into a repulsive caricature of what he probably meant as a smug smile. "I brought a guest with me, somebody who has something to say to you." He gestured, and a man stepped out from around the corner. "I poked around and discovered you had a brother. Interesting story he had to tell about you, and about how you left him."

Everything stopped. My ears rang with silence while dark spots danced through my vision.

All at once the grip of shock fractured and my lips pulled into a big smile. I took a step toward my brother. "Brandon! It's so good to see you."

"Buffy."

I threw my arms around his neck, closed my eyes and held him close. I was five when Brandon was born, but when I headed off to college he'd been an inch taller than me. Now, a decade later, I had to stand on tiptoe to hug him. I was so happy he was standing in front of me I was shaking. I hadn't realized how much I'd missed my little brother until now.

It took a few, elation-filled moments to realize he wasn't returning my embrace. I forced myself to let go of him and took a step back. I looked into his sweet face, now thinner and longer and covered with five o'clock shadow. I would have been happy to just stand there and look at him for hours. "How are you?"

"Same old, same old." He held my gaze, and I saw pain in the dark hazel depths of his eyes. "You know how it is."

I swallowed so hard it hurt my suddenly dry throat. There was anger in his expression, anger he was certainly entitled to.

"Why didn't you return my phone calls?"

He shrugged. "I thought you'd be too busy with your big important job."

"I'm never too busy for you. Please, call me anytime."

He just looked at me, his expression bland. Only his eyes betrayed the pain and anger I caused when I went away to college. "I'll keep that in mind."

The sound of footsteps caught my attention, and relief flooded me. "Maddie, Liza, this is my brother. Brandon, this is my good friend and roommate Madison and her friend Liza."

Maddie smiled and held out her hand. "So you're Brandon. I've heard a lot about you."

His eyes opened in surprise for a second, then his forehead pulled into a frown. "Buffy talks about me?"

"*Buffy?*" Liza's confused expression would be funny at another time. Tonight, it just seemed sad.

"Yeah," Butch put in, "that's her real name. And she comes from a trailer park in Alabama."

I opened my mouth to correct him, but my brother beat me to the draw. "We grew up on Keller Street. It's an exclusive upper class neighborhood that's also known as 'Snobs' Knob'. Our mother and stepfather still live there."

A harried middle-aged woman stuck her head around the corner. "Are you coming?"

Maddie's eyes widened. "We'll be right there, Mrs. Stoker."

The woman disappeared, and Maddie looked at me. "They're about to announce the winner. That's why we came to get you, so you could take pictures."

I looked at Brandon. I wanted to go somewhere and talk, but I had a responsibility. "I promised the newspaper I'd take photos. Their regular guy is out of town."

Brandon shrugged. "Whatever."

Maddie grabbed his arm. "Come with us and see the show. Then you and your sister can go out to dinner and catch up."

He didn't have a chance. Maddie was strong for an

ex-cheerleader-beauty-queen turned reporter.

We trudged out into the audience and stood near the front while the emcee cracked jokes, gave out special awards, and finally got to the runners up. By the time Lavern Walker took the crown, the tension was pitched so high it should have been possible to strum it. When the new Miss Ugly Creek walked down the aisle, the crowd went wild.

I zigzagged all over the place, getting shots of the stage, the crowd, the emcee and anything that looked interesting.

As soon as the festivities were over I hurried back toward my brother. I looked forward to spending some time with him. It took a few minutes to slip through the mass of people to get back to the side of the auditorium but I finally made it. "Where's Brandon?"

"He's gone," Liza said, frustration pulling at the corners of her mouth. "He was right beside me. I was watching the crowning, and when I looked back he was gone. She touched my arm, and I felt her regret. "I'm so sorry. I should have kept an eye on him."

"It's not your fault. He's an adult."

Wow. That's something I had never actually faced. I guess somehow I thought he'd be a kid forever. Back there in Alabama waiting for me to come home and rescue him.

But of course he grew up without me, and had an understandable load of anger aimed straight at yours truly. Well, so be it. I wanted to apologize and try to explain myself if I could. I wasn't at all sure he'd listen, but I had to try. I rushed through the building trying to find him, but both Brandon and that hateful Butch appeared to have vanished.

Eventually I was forced to admit defeat and headed back to where Liza sat and chewed on her lower lip. She saw me and rushed over. "Any luck?"

I shook my head mournfully. "Where's Maddie?"

"She's still looking for Brandon." Liza pulled out her cell. "Maddie, Stephie's here. She didn't find him." She closed her phone. "She's on her way back."

"I can't believe he's gone." I hurriedly looked away so Liza wouldn't see the tears filling my eyes. Damn! My brother shows up and then just as quickly he's gone.

Worse, that Butch idiot was involved.

"I tried, Stephie." Maddie hurried over to us, took one look at me and pulled me into her arms. "I'm sorry."

I nodded, glad that after everything, my friend was willing to hug me and give me support.

"He's around; he can't hide from us. We'll find him and lock him in a room with you so he has to listen."

"Thanks, Maddie."

We got in Liza's Silver Lexus and headed back to Margaret's house. As we went, Maddie kept glancing back over the seat. She was worried about me. Just a few hours ago she was treating me like dirt, but now she was worried. I'd be mad but I knew there was more going on here than just a girlfriend spat. Maddie, like me, had some deep-rooted issues. For her, Jake was part of the whole issue thing. For me, my brother was the symbol of all that had gone wrong with my life. We'd work it out, Maddie and me. Of that I was sure.

I wasn't so sure about Brandon and me.

Two hours later I was sitting on Margaret's

screened-in porch, staring at the screen of my laptop—and the remarkably clear picture of a Bigfoot. Incredible!

I'd always quietly made fun of the whole Bigfoot hunt thing, thinking the creatures couldn't possibly exist. After all, if something that big existed wouldn't somebody find a body, or get clear pictures of one? Like the shot on my screen right now.

Maybe things like that didn't happen because the Bigfoot creatures were smart and organized enough to not leave their bodies lying around. Maybe smart enough to speak English—which presented anthropological and physiological questions I didn't have the background to contemplate. Is it bad I was kinda happy I didn't?

It was obvious the people of Ugly Creek, or at least some of them, were being careful to keep the Bigfoot (Bigfoots, Bigfeet?)...hairy critters secret. Even as they held a Big Foot Festival every year.

I leaned back against the chair and sighed. Apparently I'd been right all along. It looked a lot like the festival was a celebration of the creatures. Likely the story about the big-footed founder *was* just a cover.

And that was yet another reason why the creatures remained hidden, there probably were towns all over the place that kept the Bigfoot secret and shielded them from the outside world.

Holy big hairy secret, Batman.

I looked out into the dark woody backyard, squinting hard, listening with everything I had, studying every tiny movement, every little noise. I longed to see or hear something that would indicate a creature that could not possibly exist, not only did, but might be just a few feet in front of me.

I wanted to see him or maybe it was a her. I wished I could talk to him, he seemed like a boy to me. I thought maybe I understood him, but what did I know?

I felt empathy for him. He was alone, different, lonely, scared, looking for his place in the world.

I realized I was crying and swiped at my face. Was I really feeling sorry for the creature, or was it myself I was crying for?

I forced away the pity party and sat up straighter in the chair. Good grief, I'd made a fantastic discovery and all I could think about was my own pathetic life. So I'd had it rough as a kid, I was far from the only one. Many folks had lived much worse childhoods than I had and still gone on to achieve incredible things. All that crap was in the past. I had to put on my big girl panties and get the hell over it.

I just hoped somehow the little brother I left behind would again be part of my life.

I heard footsteps and hurriedly clicked the Bigfoot photo off the screen.

Maddie opened the door and stepped out onto the porch. "How're you holding up?"

"I'm fine." But I looked down at my keyboard as I said it.

"You and your brother will work things out. I just know it."

"I hope so." The thought of Brandon had my eyes stinging again. How could I have gone away and left him there? How could I have left him to the monster?

But what else could I have done?

Maddie's hand touched my shoulder, and then she was gone. She probably assumed I needed time to myself to think, that was my usual MO, after all. But for once in my life, I really wanted somebody to talk to. I wanted to open up and tell another person the kinds of things that had made me run as soon as I had an opportunity, and what made me feel so bad about leaving my baby brother behind. I'm not at all sure I could have given words to the nightmare, but I kinda wished this time she'd have tried to convince me to talk.

Of course I could have gone after her, asked her to listen. And she would have. I didn't go, though. For the same reason I hadn't said anything to her about the way she'd spoken to me earlier. I was scared. Yeah, that's right, I'm a chicken. Cluck, cluck. I don't have a lot of friends, not really. I have a lot of acquaintances; there are a lot of people in my life who probably would be my friends if I knew a damn thing about how to make a friendship work. But the honest truth was I was pretty lonely most of the time. I wasn't about to do anything that would lose me the best friend I'd ever had, and hearing some of the stuff I had to tell might push her away. It wasn't worth it.

At least that was what I told myself as I closed down my computer and headed upstairs. I had a busy day planned for tomorrow, and I needed to try to sleep.

As I stepped across the threshold, I had a sudden tingling feeling on the back of my neck. I turned, but I didn't see anything in the trees.

Probably the Bigfoot, I decided. But that didn't explain the warning claxon howling in my subconscious. When I got to the bedroom I looked out again. For a second I thought I saw movement, but then it was gone.

A chill washed over me. Something just seemed off. Oh great. Now I was turning psychic. Or paranoid.

Disgusted at myself, I pulled on an oversized T-shirt and threw myself into the bed.

****

It was so dark, even the faint light of the moon didn't invade the space in which I lay. I felt for the sheet and pulled it over my shoulders. The air conditioner must be working well, because there was an actual chill in the air. It felt wonderful after the cooking I'd endured for the last few days.

Then I heard Maddie's voice, quiet, muffled, coming from the bed next to mine. And I saw the briefest glow of a tiny light. She must be on her cell phone, I decided, as I yawned and pulled the sheet tighter under my chin.

"I can't believe my own mother would lie to me like that," I heard her say. "A boyfriend, at her age. What is she thinking? And working for Jake after the way he's acted all these years. Liza knew about it, but she didn't tell me."

I stifled the groan as I rolled over and covered my head. She was talking to Greg, her mostly off again sort-of boyfriend. Personally, I didn't like the guy; he struck me as an irritating toad's behind. Sometimes, though, Maddie gave in to the urge to see him or talk to him. And I guess this was one of those times.

"I even saw Stephie kissing Jake. No kidding. Right on the tonsils. So embarrassing."

Oh great, not only was my best friend still seriously pissed at me, that slimy Greg would probably take an ad out in *The Weekly Tattler*, that cheesy tell-all paper at the checkout counter. Not the one on top, the

156

one near the bottom of the rack.

I heard a soft sob. "I can't believe the three of them have so little consideration for my feelings. Especially my own mother. Working for him. Do you believe that?"

I closed my eyes and finally dozed off to sleep, leaving Greg to stir the flame of Maddie's anger. I knew I should stay awake and talk to her after they hung up, but it was late and I was tired. Maybe I'd regret ignoring the conversation, but I was tired. Tomorrow was soon enough to deal with it. I hoped.

Chapter 12

"Those photos you emailed me yesterday are amazing. It's incredible how you captured the ambiance of the pageant. I know you have a great reputation, but I didn't expect to be so totally blown away."

"Thank you, Mr. Costa." Someone with my experience as a photographer shouldn't be blushing just because of a little praise, but the happiness in the face of this small town newspaper editor gave me the warm fuzzy tingles. I'd received serious photography awards, but that was nothing compared to the pure satisfaction of seeing someone enjoy my pictures. "Here's the disk with all the photos."

"Thank you so much for doing this."

"My pleasure." Trust me, it was.

"If you ever decided you want more from life than big city antics, I'd give you a job in a heartbeat."

I cringed at the uncomfortable pitch of my chuckle. How could an offer like that sound so good? "Wouldn't your regular photographer be upset if you gave away his job?"

"Ace only works part-time anyway. He's a big animal rescue person who takes pictures to support himself and his pack of dogs."

"Yikes, I wouldn't want to take away his income." Just thinking about it sent guilt through my heart.

"Oh, don't worry about that. He does a lot of

freelance photography while he's on the mutt rescues. Besides, he's one of Ugly Creek's own, and we'll take care of him." The editor grinned. "Doesn't mean I wouldn't love to have you join our staff."

In spite of Mr. Costa's reassurances, I left the newspaper feeling a bit guilty. Logic told me this Ace dude wasn't even in town. There was no way he could have covered the pageants. I had nothing to feel guilty about for helping the local paper in his absence.

Of course, I'm pretty sure Jake could have waited a little longer to get the shots for the website and brochure. So I did take that job from Ace whoever. Hey, it was for a good cause. The kids, remember? Sick kids in the hospital. Can't argue with that. Right?

As I walked over two streets and down a block to Blackwood Antiques, my mind turned over the idea of what it would be like to stay here in Ugly Creek. No more over-priced and over-done parties. No more catching shots of politicians and their girlfriends or boyfriends or hookers. Or even politicians just being too cozy with someone of the opposing viewpoint. No more being perpetually late because more was expected from the *Spy* employees than any mortal could do in a week, much less twenty-four hours.

I took a deep breath, and the sweet smell of honeysuckle tickled my nostrils. It would be great not to smell the acrid stench of vehicles, to be able to open my window at night. To be able to relax once in a while. To not always be searching for the one big photo opportunity. The one that could propel me from *Capitol Spy* to *The New York Times*.

I stopped right in the middle of the sidewalk, earning me a glare from a well-dressed woman who was walking way too fast to be a small town resident.

Of course I had The Shot. The one that could make my career. The Bigfoot. It was unthinkable, of course, the idea of using that shot. Even if it put me on top of the heap. Most photojournalists would.

But I'm not most photojournalists.

Truthfully, the whole idea made me want to vomit. What would happen to those beautiful creatures if I did manage to get the scientific community to believe? What would happen to Ugly Creek?

Whether one photojournalist made it to the big time wasn't nearly as important as the Bigfeet and the well-being of an odd little town.

I smiled and continued walking toward Jake's store. I'd delete the photo when I got back to Maddie's. Until then it should be fine. I'd saved it in a locked file and made the password "Feisty", the name of the dog I had when I was a kid, before my dad left. Who would know that, other than Brandon, of course? Ugly Creek's secret was safe.

I pushed open the big wooden door into Blackwood Antiques and found Jake comforting a crying Margaret. My throat filled with fear as I rushed over to the counter. "What happened?"

"I'm just a big old weepy mess today. I'm sorry."

She sat back and wiped her eyes, but Jake didn't move from where he sat next to her, his arm around her back, his frown locked on her face. "She hurt your feelings."

Margaret's smile was weak, forced. "Children and parents are supposed to hurt each other's feelings. That's just the way things are."

Oh boy. "What did Maddie do?"

Margaret sniffled and wiped at her nose with a tissue. "She didn't mean it. She's still hurting. It's hard for a girl to lose her father."

Jake's gaze dropped to the counter, and I saw him swallow. "Maddie said Margaret was a traitor to her own daughter because she works for me."

I sucked in air. This was not good. I couldn't believe Maddie had spoken to her mother that way. Something was very wrong here, and I had a feeling Greg had a lot to do with instigating it.

"It's okay, Jake," Margaret said.

"No, it's not." Jake stood and turned away, his fists gripped, his jaw muscles clenched. "It's me she has a problem with. She has no right to take it out on you."

"But—"

"*No.*" Jake closed his eyes, and his entire body tensed for a moment. Then his shoulders dropped and he turned to Margaret. He gently cupped her chin with his hand. "I won't have you dragged into this crap. If Madison has a problem with me then she should come to me." His gaze dropped to the counter. "But we all know she's a coward."

Margaret's eyes all but popped out of her head and she was on her feet before I could blink. "Jacob Blackwood! I will not have you talking about my daughter that way."

"I'm sorry, Margaret, but it's the truth." With that, he stomped off into the back. I heard his footsteps as they went up the stairs and then across the floor into his apartment.

"One of these days I'm going to turn the both of them over my knees."

Margaret stood, arms crossed tightly in front of

her, glaring in the direction Jake had gone with an intensity I honestly thought would blow a hole in the back wall.

I swallowed hard and made a mental note to be careful never to get on her bad side. I was pretty sure I'd rather face down a big old hungry Grizzly than that woman when she was pissed.

And she was thoroughly pissed at the moment.

An idea that had been wandering through my head for a few days popped to the surface. It was a crazy idea, and could just as likely make things worse as to solve anything. But Maddie and I were heading back to D.C. soon. I only had a short amount of time to try to do something about the Clark-Blackwood feud. Maybe, just maybe, it was worth a try. I could at least see what Margaret had to say about it.

Ten minutes later, Margaret stared at me with a face so expressionless I was afraid I'd upset her more. Which was definitely not what I was aiming for. I shrugged and tried to look nonchalant. "It was just an idea."

Her lips slowly curled upward. "One that just might work."

A relief wave wiped the muscle tension from my body, leaving me limp. I dropped onto the stool beside her. "You think so?"

She shrugged. "Who knows with those two, but it's the best idea I've heard in a while. Actually, it's the *only* idea I've heard in a long time."

She squeezed my hand. "I think we should at least give your plan a try. If you're serious about this, then I'll talk to Henry at lunchtime. He can help, and he has a backroom where we can set things up."

Margaret's enthusiasm stoked mine, and I found myself getting excited about the possibility my crazy plan might just work. "I should see Liza and Steve tonight. I'll try to run the idea past at least one of them." I had a gut feeling they would be willing to help.

"If everything goes okay, we can put things in motion after the parade tomorrow."

"Works for me." I looked at my watch and gasped. "I'd better get going. I told Maddie I'd meet her at the craft fair. If I don't go now I won't have time to look at anything before she gets there."

Margaret smiled knowingly. "Crafts are not really Madison's thing."

"Not so much, no." I gave Margaret a quick hug and kiss on the cheek, then hurried out the door. This had to work, it just had to!

It seemed darker outside than when I'd arrived in town just a couple of hours before. The steam bath humidity made the hot day feel just that much hotter. I headed up Main Street and across Market to the courthouse square where the band played a few days before.

I couldn't keep from taking a quick peek up at the sky but there was no sign of strange glowing objects flying overhead. What I did see were clouds that seemed to be getting darker by the minute. I checked my watch and saw Maddie was supposed to meet me in about a half hour. The warning smell of water in the air had me wondering which would be worse: the heat, or the rain. Probably it would be the increased heat and humidity after the rain ended. Sighing, I pulled out my cell phone.

Maddie didn't answer her phone so I headed over

to check out the crafts. She might have figured out rain was headed this way and was about to cut my enjoyment short.

There was an amazing variety of crafts. Crochet, needlepoint, homemade candles, wooden silhouettes to put in the yard, and the ubiquitous—but nevertheless beautiful—patchwork quilts. I smiled, remembering my grandmother Grace showing me the quilt she'd made of pieces from her children's outgrown and tattered clothing. It was an amazing work of art, filled with memories and love. Grandma, my father's mother, had willed it to me, and I had carefully spread it on my bed, moved beyond words by the gesture.

Two weeks later I'd come home from school to find the quilt replaced by a brand new bedspread. I'd run to find my mother and ask her what happened to my precious quilt. She said she didn't want that cheap ugly thing in her house. It didn't go with the décor, she'd said. She'd thrown it out. Yeah, she had a thing about what was on my bed, and I had little else to decorate. No *Pirates of the Caribbean* posters on my walls.

I'd screamed at her, knowing even as I did I'd be in trouble for disrespect but I didn't care. She'd disrespected me, my grandmother, and my heritage. I hated her then, really, truly hated her. When my stepdad got home, he left welts and bruises but I didn't cry. I knew I was right.

I cried for a month but never when Mom or my stepdad could see me. I didn't want to give them the satisfaction.

I've never stopped hating either of them.

"Are you all right?"

I looked up to see the quilt vendor standing beside

me. I looked down and tears fell onto the quilt I was caressing. I quickly wiped my eyes. "I'm sorry, I was remembering my grandmother."

"You really miss her."

I nodded, afraid to speak lest the tears start again.

The woman touched my arm. "Your memories keep her alive."

I nodded again, forced a watery smile, and headed over to check out the jewelry.

I tried a couple more times to call Maddie, but she wasn't answering. The sky didn't seem to be getting any worse, so I threw myself into enjoying the fair. Not that it was hard, mind you. Not with all the gorgeous things on sale.

I bought a necklace and matching earrings, and a few minutes later I snagged a hand-knitted green and gold shawl that would look perfect with my green fall dress. Not practical maybe, but I loved it.

The rain blew in on a gust of wind. Hard and instantly chilling, it had people squealing and hustling to cover wares and purchases. Everybody rushed in different directions, trying either to find a dry place to wait out the storm, or their cars so they could head for home.

I sprinted down the street, finally managing to find a hidey hole in a doorway, although the overhang did little to keep out the blowing rain. I turned to face the back, pulled out my cell and tried once again to call Madison, but there was still no answer.

Thunder echoed between the canyon of buildings, and I decided I didn't want to stand here indefinitely. I'd instinctively run back across Market to Main, so it was a short run from there to Misty Lane.

165

"Stephie?" Margaret said as I dashed in, bringing rain and wind with me. "My goodness, you're soaked!"

"Jake." She yelled, then rushed over to me. "You poor thing."

Jake came out of the back, and Margaret turned to him. "Why don't you take Stephie upstairs and get her some towels?"

By this time, Margaret had edged me professionally into the middle of the shop, where Jake snagged me by the arm. "Come with me," he said.

A handful of customers eyed us, and I tried to ignore them as I was guided toward the back.

We headed up the steps, and into Jake's apartment. "I'll get you something to wear and put your clothes in the dryer."

I nodded and followed him into his bedroom. The bedroom, where we'd made love just a couple of days before. I shivered, and not just from the air conditioner blowing on my wet body.

"These are way too big, but they should work until your things are dry." He handed me a T-shirt and a pair of sweatpants. Then he walked out and closed the door behind him.

As I undressed, I debated leaving on my bra and panties, but wet undies were more uncomfortable than wet outer clothes. So I stripped, dried off, put on the soft sweats that were probably six sizes too big but at least were equipped with a drawstring, and dried my hair with the other towel. Ah, much better. I was warm again.

There was a soft knock, and Jake peeked around the edge of the door. "Decent?"

"Sometimes. I'm dressed, by the way."

He chuckled and walked into the room.

Abruptly I became very aware of my lack of undies. I could feel the cotton material of the shirt rub against my nipples. Jake's clothes. That thought led very quickly to the idea of Jake's hands. I swallowed so hard I think I scratched my throat.

"You're adorable."

I looked at him. His expression didn't say adorable. His face seemed to tell another story altogether. Something closer to spice than sweet.

He moved closer, and I saw his eyes were dark; his chest moved with quickly inhaled and exhaled air, the artery in his neck pulsed.

My knees got weak.

Jake pulled me close and touched his lips to mine. I pretty much collapsed against him. "I want you," I whispered. "Take me."

He pulled his clothes off my body and lowered me to the bed. His hands caressed, his lips kissed, his body lit fires wherever it touched mine. I pulled at his shirt while he whispered sweet somethings in my ear. Now normally I'm a little shy, but I knew what this man could do to me, and I wanted a repeat performance.

Before I had time to consider the consequences.

He stood long enough to strip off his clothes and pull on a condom, and then he was back on top of me. And I couldn't think at all. All I could do was feel. Trust me. That was enough.

The storm had long passed by the time I'd showered, my clothes had dried, and I grabbed my shoulder bag and headed down the stairs. An annoying beeping sound seemed to be following me as I went. By the time I reached the bottom, I'd figured out the sound was coming from my cell phone. I fished it out and listened to the messages. It was Maddie wondering where I was. I looked at the incoming calls and saw her number listed ten times. Oh boy!

I quickly dialed her.

"Where are you? I've been worried."

"I'm sorry, Maddie. I got caught in the storm and had to find shelter. Besides, I tried to call you about a million times."

"I'm at the courthouse square, where are you?"

*Busted.* "At Blackwood Antiques."

There was the sound of a sharp intake of air. "I'll meet you out front."

The phone clicked as I took the three more steps onto the main floor. I went over to the counter and leaned against it. "Oh boy."

Margaret put a hand on my shoulder. "Are you all right?"

"I just got off the phone with Maddie. She's picking me up out front."

She sighed and shook her head sadly. "If my daughter gives you too much grief, you let me know. I'd be happy to turn her over my knee."

She turned to greet a customer, and I chewed on my bottom lip to keep from smiling. Twice in one day she'd threatened to spank her big baby. I knew she'd do it too. Maddie was taller than her mom, but Margaret would find a way, of that I was sure. It was obvious she felt Maddie was acting like a child. I gotta say, I pretty much agreed. But then, I wasn't exactly acting like a responsible adult lately either.

The sun was out, and I knew it would only take minutes for Maddie to get there, so I gathered my things and cornered Jake. "I have to go," I told him.

I saw sadness in his warm, caring expression. "I really enjoyed today."

"Me too." I stared up into those hot obsidian eyes. I didn't want to go. I wanted to head back upstairs, crawl back into his bed, and make love until sometime next week.

"Will I see you again?"

Reality swept through me with more intensity than the earlier storm. It wouldn't be long before I had to go back to my job, my life. "Yes," I whispered. "Yes, you will."

"I'll be looking forward to it."

His kiss was gentle, but the passion that sparked through it all but incinerated me on the spot. No other man would ever make me feel quite the way this one did, of that I was sure. I believe I'd have traded everything I'd worked for if I could just go back up those steps with him.

Then he pulled back, and I saw the regret in his eyes. It couldn't be, and we both knew it.

"See you around," I whispered, and he nodded.

I turned and all but ran out, sure if I slowed down, even a little, I'd never go. I fought the tears, but a few leaked out in spite of my efforts.

Less than three minutes later, Maddie pulled up to the curb. I jumped in and she took off before I had my seatbelt buckled. "You don't look like you got caught in the storm."

"Margaret made sure I got dried off."

"Sounds like her."

And then it was quiet.

To amuse myself, and keep my mind off the man

I'd just walked away from, I watched the houses go by. Just like back home in Crooked Hollow, it was common for a large expensive house to sit right beside a tiny one. This mix seemed to be a peculiarity of the South, though both moneyed and not knew their places well. Maybe that's why it worked in the South; knowing one's place was a basic Southern trait.

One thing did surprise me; here there didn't seem to be the kind of severe poverty I'd seen back home. There were no shacks, no 1970s' trailer homes with broken windows and overgrown yards. No dirty kids in nothing but diapers, playing with secondhand toys in the yard.

I thought again of what the editor of the local paper had said, "We take care of our own." Maybe they really did. That would be refreshing, uplifting.

Actually, that would be freaking amazing.

I was wondering what it would be like to live in a place like that when I saw it. "Perfect."

"What's perfect?"

"That house." Happy she'd spoken to me, I pointed toward the modest brick rancher with a for sale sign in front.

She was frowning. "Perfect for what?"

I was beginning to wish I hadn't said anything. But then, Maddie was my closest friend. If I couldn't talk to her, who could I talk to? "It's silly, but that house is exactly the kind I'd like to live in one day."

She gave me a confused look, then shrugged. "Maybe you can find something similar near D.C."

The realization that I didn't want to move anywhere near D.C. scared me a little. Okay, maybe it scared me a lot. I was getting way too attached to this weird little town. What in the world was wrong with me? I'd set my goals in the ninth grade and hadn't looked back.

Until now.

We went back to quiet, contemplative traveling, and I thought about how Maddie wasn't happy with me just for being in Jake's store. How would she feel if she knew I'd been in his bed? Twice. And what would she think if she knew I was actually giving thought to what it would be like to live here. What it would be like to be married—

Oh hell no! I was so not going down that road. Down that way was total, complete, insanity. Nope. Not going.

Stephie Blackwood. It did have a nice sound.

Stop, brain. No. Never happen. Not in a million years. My best friend hates him.

Maybe the plan would work.

Or not. Be realistic! I screamed at my brain.

The car stopped, and I had been so wrapped up in my guilty ruminations I hadn't realized we had arrived at Margaret's house.

Maddie said nothing to me, just grabbed her purse and headed toward the door. Kicking myself mentally, I took off after her.

She headed into the kitchen, dumped her purse on a chair, and poured herself a glass of orange juice. "We're planning to leave for the carnival about five."

"Maddie, I'm sorry about going to Jake's to get out of the storm. I should have gone somewhere else."

She shrugged. "Doesn't matter. My mom works there, after all."

Her voice squeaked, and I knew the tightness was

due to barely held in emotions. Oddly, that made me a little angry. "I did try to call you," I pointed out. "Repeatedly."

She dropped into a chair. "I'm sorry I stranded you. I just got to thinking and lost track of time. Then the storm hit and you didn't answer."

"Thinking?"

"Yeah. About my life." She picked at the design on the tablecloth. "Dani Phillips was at the brunch this morning."

"Your old rival? You tangled for the job of school newspaper editor, right?"

"Yeah. I won." Her face lit for a second, then drooped again. "She's lost a lot of weight and she's got gorgeous curly hair like you. She's beautiful."

Huh? Me? My gorgeous what?

"The worst thing is that she just landed a job with *The New York Times*. Do you believe it? Everybody always said I was a much better writer than her, but here I am working at *Spy* that's one step above tabloid, and she's with the freaking *New York Times*." She groaned and lowered her face into her hands.

I just sat and stared at her. This development was too shocking for words. For emotions, even.

"What happened to the life I had planned?"

Okay, enough with the drama queen. "Wait a minute. I'm the insecure one. You're the freaking ex-cheerleader! What's going on here?"

She peeked out at me from between her fingers. "Coming back here just shook me up, I guess. In my daydreams I always imagined I'd return like some conquering hero, but I'm just a reporter. Big deal. *Dani Phillips* is the conquering hero."

My brain was going to explode. I rubbed my throbbing forehead and worked at assimilating what I was hearing. "But, you always said you loved working in D.C. Finger on the pulse of the country and all that."

"I did. I do. I don't know." She groaned.

This was. Just. Too. Weird. "Maddie, you're a respected reporter at a major magazine that reports on the running of our country. You're gorgeous, you're smart, you're talented. What more do you want?"

She let out a long, pathetic sigh. "I don't know."

I leaned back in my chair. "Maybe the carnival will cheer you up."

"Maybe so." She sniffed delicately. "I guess we should start getting ready."

I started to get out of my chair, but she was faster. "I'm first in the shower," she yelled, as she headed for the stairs.

I sat back down. How did she always do that? I grabbed her untouched orange juice and downed it. I couldn't believe Maddie doubted herself. She was the one who'd kept me on track for the last few years. Without Madison Clark, I don't think I could have survived the city and the back stabbing I'd landed in when I accepted the job for *Capitol Spy*. If Maddie was having doubts, what chance did I have of being sure what I was doing?

At least I was too freaked to feel guilty over my latest sleeping-with-her-enemy stunt, but I knew that wasn't going to last long.

Chapter 13

Apparently, carnivals are the same everywhere. I find that observation oddly reassuring.

As I walked through the Ugly Creek Big Foot Festival Carnival (courtesy of a traveling carnival company), I felt like I was seventeen again and at the Crooked Hollow yearly carnival with my boyfriend at the time. I really cared for the guy, but my family argued he wasn't good enough, which insulted his family. We tried, but the pressure was just too great, and eventually we broke up.

I ambled between the concession trailers and the booths where a guy could try to impress his date by paying a fortune to accomplish a damn near impossible task and collecting the bounty of a stuffed animal. Smiling, I watched one scrawny dude throw a wooden ring around the proper cone and hand his admiring girlfriend a pink pig. This was fun.

Two seconds later, I stepped in a mud puddle and changed my mind.

"I love the smell of cotton candy," Liza said.

I turned to greet the group, who had gone to check out the rides while I sniffed out the games and prizes section.

Steve raised an eyebrow. "You do know that stuff is straight-up sugar, right?"

Liza gave her husband a smacking shove to the

shoulder with her un-casted arm. "Bite me."

"Oh, look. There's Tina," Maddie said.

With junior-high squeals, Liza and Maddie took off in Tina's direction.

"You're evil," I told Steve.

He grinned. "Hey, I was just pointing out the obvious."

Since Maddie and Liza were busy chatting with this Tina person and her buddies, I edged closer to Steve. "I have something I'd like to talk to you about."

He adjusted his glasses. "Okay."

"This thing with Maddie and Jake."

His forehead pulled into an unsure frown. "What about it?"

Sudden nerves had my knees shaking, but I plowed on. "I think they just need to sit down and talk."

Steve sighed. "I've been trying to tell Jake that for years."

"Well, I was thinking… if we could… maybe *convince* them to talk."

The slight shake of his head and the amused pull of his lips told me what he thought of the idea. "You do know those two are possibly the most stubborn people in the Western Hemisphere?"

I swallowed. "That's why I was thinking of something a little. Well, drastic."

His eyebrows shot up so high they were visible above the frame of his glasses. "I'm listening."

By the time Liza and Maddie returned from their chat with Tina and friends, Steve had a cat-eating-mouse expression on his face, and I was beginning to think there might be hope for my crazy plan.

Three hours later, I was seriously sick of being the

proverbial third wheel, or fourth, I guess, in this case. Maddie, Liza, and Steve had a past in common, and a good part of the time, I felt like I was eavesdropping. I didn't know enough to care about the people they talked about, and I didn't understand half of what they were talking about anyway. Eventually my comfort level passed wearisome and smacked right into depressing.

"I'm going to look around over here," I told them. Maddie nodded vaguely, Liza didn't seem to notice, and Steve gave me a sheepish grin. Poor guy, I don't think his comfort level was much higher than mine.

I wandered around for a while, taking in the ambiance. The sun was setting, and the lights edging the rides were flickering on. The Ferris wheel looked especially awesome, with the brilliant reds and purples of sunset forming a backdrop for the lofty structure.

"Wanna ride?"

I knew he was behind me before he spoke, but it didn't change the intense flash of desire his voice provoked in me. "No, thank you," I said, my voice strained.

"What's wrong?" Jake asked. "Chicken?"

I shrugged. "I don't like heights."

"I'll protect you."

I turned to glare at him. "From the thing collapsing and killing us all?"

"Yep."

I unbuttoned a middle button and pulled open his shirt a bit. He gave me a wondering frown and I smiled. "Just looking for your Superman costume."

"We could go back to my place and look for other things."

I carefully fastened his shirt back before longing overrode my guilt and I did something I would hate myself for not regretting in the morning. "I can't."

He put two fingers under my chin and lifted it so our gazes met. "I know you're in an awkward position, and I feel bad that I had anything to do with putting you there. But I'm not the one who tore out of town ten years ago."

"Talk to her, Jake. See if you can't work things out." My voice cracked, and I knew he could see the tears forming in my eyes, but I didn't allow myself to care. This was too important.

"It was Maddie who caused the problem, not me."

"Then tell her that. Tell her how you feel."

"That would just make things worse."

I held his gaze. "You don't know that."

He closed his eyes for a moment, head down, shoulders slumped. When he met my gaze, I knew his answer. "I'm sorry," he whispered, then turned and walked away.

It took every bit of strength I had not to follow him. He wasn't like any other man I'd ever met, and my heart longed for him as much as my body did. Damn you, Jake Blackwood.

Then I turned and headed off to find my friend. Maddie would be in my life long after Jake was a distant memory. I had to remember that.

I found Maddie, Liza, and Steve outside the haunted house ride. "My husband's a chicken," Liza told me.

"I just don't like things jumping out at me. You and Maddie and Stephie go on, I'll wait out here."

"I'll wait with you," I told Steve.

Maddie frowned toward me. "I thought you loved haunted houses."

"I'm just not in the mood, okay?" Which was true. I was in the mood to beat the bloody hell out of something, and I figured a random mechanical spook jumping out might just provoke the fight or flight instinct—and I wasn't in the mood to run. I'd hate to have to pay to repair the thing.

Maddie shrugged, grabbed Liza's arm, and they took off into the spooky façade.

"Thanks for hanging with me."

I managed a smile for Steve. "Thanks for agreeing to help with the plan."

He adjusted his glasses. "Jake is my best friend and Maddie's Liza's. I'd love to not be caught in the middle." He looked at me. "And I'll bet you would too."

There was something in his expression that caught my attention. "So you know?"

He nodded. "Jake told me the two of you have something going, and that you're fighting it for all you're worth because of loyalty to Maddie. That's a tough situation to be in."

"Maddie's my friend. She has to come first."

"Even if it means breaking two hearts?"

"Whatever Jake and I have, it isn't our hearts that are involved."

"Are you sure about that?"

Was I? I turned to watch as Liza and Maddie's cart came roaring out of the house. They spilled out and headed toward us, laughing as they went.

"It might be a good idea to know what it is you feel for Jake before you make a decision that's going to affect both your lives." Steve stood and went to meet his wife. I watched as he kissed Liza, and a little ball of pain swelled in my stomach. Was he right? Were Jake and I tangled up romantically as well as physically?

"What's up with you?" Maddie asked. "You look like you did the night you caught that senator's aide and his blow-up "friend."

The memory had my stomach cringing. "Just got something on my mind."

"Well chill, girlfriend. We're on vacation." She gave me a little punch on the arm, and the four of us headed toward the tilt-a-whirl and rides beyond.

We were shaken, stirred, and flipped upside down a few times. Then we capped off the day with hotdogs and caramel apples. I was exhausted, half-nauseous, and more than ready to climb into bed. It had been a wild day.

On our way toward the entrance, we caught up with Tina and her huge, totally bald boyfriend. "You guys going home?"

"Yep." Liza looped her good arm around Tina. "We've had just about enough of junk food and wild rides. You too?"

Tina laughed. "What can I say? Gotta have my beauty sleep."

I found myself hoping her beauty sleep would also make her high pitched laugh more palpable, but I managed to keep my big mouth shut. Barely. Did I mention she had a huge boyfriend?

Tina walked with us toward the street where we'd parked. We were just outside the perimeter of the actual carnival when I spotted Jake walking a few feet ahead of us. Even in the dappled glow of the streetlights filtering through the leaves on the trees, his hard body had my heart beating faster.

I realized Madison had stopped when I plowed into her. "Maddie?" When she didn't answer, I followed her gaze right to Jake. The expression on her face was one of pain and longing, and my conscience glared at me.

"Maddie and Jake, the magic couple. I always thought they'd be together forever," Tina's stage whisper reached me.

Immediately I saw tears form in Maddie's eyes. Holy Maloney, or holy-something-more-bad-wordy.

Jake disappeared around a corner and Maddie came out of her trance and started walking again. The rest of us began to move along with her.

"I had so much junk food I'm afraid to look in the mirror tomorrow," Liza said.

"Fat and processed sugar, horrible for the human body," Steve said.

Liza glared at him. "You ate three times as much as I did."

He shrugged. "Just because the stuff's bad for you doesn't mean I don't want any."

"Hypocrite."

"Am not." He made to grab her, but Liza took off running, laughing as she went. Steve caught her a half block up the way. They wrestled a minute, then grabbed each other and dove into a kiss that had parents covering little kids' eyes. Actually, I kind of felt like covering my own eyes.

"Get a room," Tina told them.

I didn't say anything, but I had to agree with the sentiment.

Tina and Huge took off toward their car, and the

rest of us piled into the hot couple's gorgeous black Lexus and headed for home. Steve and Liza were busy making plans for later that I didn't want to think about. Maddie stared out the window without saying a word. And I sat and worried. I was so in over my head.

Then again, what else was new?

Chapter 14

"What did you do to my computer?"

I stopped halfway between the hallway and the bedroom. "What are you talking about?"

Maddie pointed to her screen. "It was booted up and on standby. I closed it down yesterday after I checked my email."

I wrapped the towel around my hair and went over to her laptop. "Are you sure?"

"Positive."

"I haven't touched it. Let me check mine."

She frowned. "Why?"

I simply shrugged. Something told me she wouldn't want to hear my reasoning. "Mine's on standby too."

"Maybe Mom used mine. She could have tried yours first, then realized it wasn't mine."

"Maybe." Honestly, I doubted it. I really didn't think it would be hard to figure out the pink one was Maddie's. Mine was black, had a bigger screen, and more RAM. I had some serious photo software on mine, plus the photos stored on the hard drive. And mine was password protected. It was highly unlikely Margaret could get into my computer even if she tried. And why the heck would she even want to?

I did a quick check to see if I could figure out what someone besides me might have gotten into, but

Maddie was giving me quizzical looks, so I decided to go in another direction. "Let's go ask your mother if she used our computers."

As we went downstairs, I decided in spite of the total, complete unlikelihood of it happening, I seriously hoped Margaret had, for some unknown reason, booted up and managed to get into my computer. I wasn't crazy about anybody using my computer. On the other hand, any other explanation was beyond scary.

"Mom, did you use my computer?" Maddie asked as soon as we got to the kitchen doorway.

Margaret frowned. "No. Is something wrong?"

Maddie dropped into a chair at the kitchen table. "My computer was on standby mode and I always shut it down completely."

"You didn't forget just one time? After all, you're on vacation. And a bit stressed out." Margaret gave her daughter a look that said she knew the stress was more than a "bit."

"Stephie's was on standby too. And she keeps hers locked up like Fort Knox." Maddie grinned and glanced toward me. "She's paranoid, but I know how to get in there."

I'd pulled myself onto a barstool. "I'm not paranoid, just used to keeping important shots and expensive software safe. And yeah, you know me well enough to get in my computer, and Brandon could too, probably. He knows the passwords I like and how I tend to set things up." This talk of my brother was making me sad. "Bottom line, no, I didn't accidentally leave my computer on. I finished up the shots for the newspaper, put them on a disk, and shut everything down. There's no way I forgot." I shifted a little.

"Besides, what are the odds Maddie and I would forget to shut down our computers on the same day?"

"True." Margaret's face pulled into a deep-thinking frown and she walked over to the back door. "I always take my morning coffee on the porch, but this morning the lock wasn't fastened. You didn't happen to go out there last night, did you, Stephie?"

"No, I went straight to bed."

"Are you saying what I think you're saying?" Maddie's eyes widened until they looked a bit like softballs. "Because break-ins don't happen in Ugly Creek. Back in high school we used to call the sheriff the Maytag Man because he never did anything."

Margaret lowered herself into one of the kitchen chairs. "Even Ugly Creek has changed in the last ten years."

"Why would someone break in and get on our laptops and not just take them?" I asked.

"Good question," Margaret said. "As far as I can tell, nothing's missing."

"You looked?" Maddie asked. Margaret nodded, and Maddie's eyes got big again. "You already thought somebody broke in."

Margaret shrugged. "I thought it was a possibility, but there was no evidence of anything. Not really. A few things seemed looked through, but nothing I could definitely say had been touched."

"We need to call the sheriff." Maddie grabbed the cordless.

I took it from her hand. "And tell him what? That somebody didn't take our computers."

"They can do fingerprints and DNA and all that stuff from TV."

"Or they'll dismiss us as paranoid," Margaret said. "Why don't we just lock up carefully, hide the laptops, or give them to me to take to work, and we'll see if anything else happens."

"Works for me," I told her.

"I'll hide my laptop here," Maddie said, in a voice so dry it made me thirsty.

My conscience twitched. "Me too," I said. I'd have felt better if my laptop was safe at Jake's store, but it wasn't worth hurting my friend over.

Maddie and I put our laptops and their cases under some clothes in storage boxes in the linen closet, and headed off to the day's festivities.

The Ugly Creek Big Foot Festival Parade started lining up on a back street at eleven am, three full hours before the two pm scheduled start time. It was a fun atmosphere, and excitement seemed to sparkle despite the inevitable last minute hitches.

In spite of the heat—and it was hot and humid enough to turn ice cream into soup—the crowd was big enough to have my heart bouncing hard in my chest. I'd have liked to curl up in a corner and hide, but I was determined. I wasn't about to let my uneasiness in crowds team up with anxiety about the laptops, and mix with the straight-up fear about whether my plan would work. That was a recipe sure to ruin my day.

I ran around lending a helping hand where I could, but mostly I took advantage of the myriad photo opportunities. The tiny bumblebees were there, along with their fairy princess dance school classmates. Business-suited dignitaries stood in the shade, jackets off, ties loosened, chatting and laughing with leather-clad equestrians who easily kept their beautiful horses calm in the neatly lined-up pandemonium.

Keeping busy kept my mind off my fear of crowds while denial held back worry about my soon to be executed crazy plan, but anxiety over what was going on with the computers spilled over in spite of my best efforts. It didn't make sense someone broke in and just booted up our computers. Unless he was looking for something. Why anybody would look for anything on our computers was beyond me. It wasn't like we were spies or something. There was nothing on either of our laptops worth breaking in over.

Except one incredible picture.

Maybe the Bigfoot broke in for it?

I chuckled. I really was getting paranoid. Nobody even knew that photo was on my computer, not even the Sasquatch-type critters.

The little bumblebee dancers were practicing their act, and I ran to watch—I mean I hurried to catch some great shots. Okay, okay, I mostly wanted to watch. They were incredibly cute little kids.

I was about halfway there when I saw my brother standing over to one side, near that jackass Butch. "Brandon!" I yelled, as I started toward him.

He looked at me, glanced toward Butch, back at me, then took off running in the opposite direction. My mouth dropped open in disbelief. I couldn't believe it. My little brother was running from me?

Determined to catch him, I sprinted off in the direction he'd gone. Out of the corner of my eye, I saw Butch's evil smirk. I should have known. Later, dude, I promised. I'd get that ass-wipe. It was just a matter of time.

Anger and determination fueled my adrenaline, and

I tore through the crowd and across the courthouse lawn. I knew Brandon wasn't happy I'd left him in Alabama, but why run away? Was I that vile?

The toe of my sandal caught a crack in the sidewalk, and suddenly I was facedown. I glanced up to see my baby brother rounding a corner. Groaning, I looked down at my equipment. The only camera I had out of the bag was my Nikon digital, and it seemed there were enough bags and things around my neck to cushion against the concrete, because there wasn't a scratch on it.

"Are you all right, dear?"

I looked up into the concerned eyes of Aunt Octavia. She was dressed in a bright red pantsuit and a hat to match. All I could think was it was good to see a friendly face. "The cameras and I are fine."

"Your leg is bleeding."

*Huh?* I looked down and sure enough, I had scraped my knee, the same one as when the Rabbit tried to take me out. Peachy. "It's just a scratch, no biggie."

"It'll get infected if it's not cared for."

I couldn't resist. "Psychic vision?"

Her smile was just a touch wily. "Common sense, actually."

I pulled myself to my feet. At least I was wearing shorts so I hadn't literally shown my butt. "I'll be fine, honest."

"Come with me." She grabbed my arm, and all but dragged me up the street. I thought about trying to resist, but I didn't want to hurt her feelings. Not to mention, the woman had quite a grip for someone her age.

We went into Ugly Drugs—which, of course, begs

the ridiculous question: what exactly are the standards of beauty for pills and such—and she hauled me toward the back. A chubby little man in a white coat rushed out from behind the pharmacy counter when he saw us. "My, that's a nasty scrape you have there, young lady."

"It's not really that bad," I protested. All this attention was embarrassing.

"You don't want it to get infected," he said.

"Get me supplies and I'll fix it up for her," Aunt Octavia said.

I was shoved into one of the fake-wood-framed green-plastic-upholstered seats where folks waited for their prescriptions. The pharmacist, Carl Mallory, his nametag said, handed Aunt Octavia items as she worked. They'd obviously done this before, their movements precise and clinical, rather like a very odd surgery scene.

When I was bandaged and both my caregivers were satisfied, I smiled toward Mr. Mallory. "How much do I owe you for the supplies?"

"You don't owe me anything. We take care of our own around here," he said.

There it was again. "But I'm not from here. I live in D.C. I'm going back there in just a few days."

"You belong here with us," Octavia said. "Isn't that right, Carl?"

"Absolutely." He gave me a big smile, then turned and headed back to his spot behind the high pharmacy counter to see to an incoming customer.

"If you're all fixed up, then I need to get going. I don't wanna miss the festivities."

I glanced at my watch. "The parade doesn't start for another two hours."

"I didn't say anything about a parade, now did I?" She gave me a wink, and I walked with her out the door and back into the crush of human craziness.

We walked together back toward the parade prep area. We were about halfway there when Aunt Octavia stopped. "This is where I get off, there's gonna be a catfight over on Magnolia Avenue in a few minutes, and I'm pulling for Margie Lane. That Betsy Smythe woman is a real bitch."

She started to turn, then froze for a moment in a way I knew all too well. She turned back to me, and I braced myself for the coming pronouncement.

"You and those you love are headed for betrayal, fear, and peril. It is your choice that will determine the outcome. Remember to follow your heart."

I stared for a moment and then forced a half-hearted smile. "Got any specifics?"

She held her hands out in surrender. "I can only pass on what the spirits tell me."

"Thanks for your help, Ms....um..."

"Call me Aunt Octavia, hon. Everybody does."

"Well, thank you, Aunt Octavia." Before I realized what was happening I was hugging the tiny woman with a huge heart.

I stepped back, and she pushed an unruly curl back from my face. "You'll be fine, dear. You only need to have faith in yourself. Now I have to go, the fight's about to start."

She headed out, and I went in the direction of the preparation area. I wasn't at all surprised when I heard somebody yell, "Fight." That woman was unfathomable.

"Want to share?"

Jake's voice had tingly warmth rushing through my body. "Share?"

"Whatever has you smiling like that."

"Aunt Octavia. She's something else."

"She's something all right."

There were darker feelings than pleasure in Jake's eyes. Crap, I forgot about the Aunt Octavia channeling his mother thing.

"What happened to your knee?"

Grateful for the distraction, I filled him in. "I saw Brandon, but the little brat ran from me. I went after him and wound up taking a header to the sidewalk."

"Are you okay?"

"I'm fine. Aunt Octavia and the pharmacist dude fixed me up. I was worried about my cameras, but they seem to be fine."

A big, warm hand brushed my face and ended up behind my neck. "The hell with the cameras, I'm just glad you're okay."

I looked up into dark eyes that seemed to flash caring. Oh, boy. Lust I could deal with, but protectiveness? Not so much into that. Still, it sort of felt good to have this big lug look at me like that. Hey, he was getting closer and closer and...his lips touched mine. Oh my, the big lug could kiss!

I felt the change in his body seconds before he backed away. My eyes opened and I saw the tension in his jaw, the flaring of his nostrils, the way his gaze was locked hard on a point somewhere behind me. I knew before I turned I would see Madison. I was ashamed she'd seen me, but her attention seemed to be solely on Jake. It was as if I wasn't even there. I'd disappeared, rendered invisible by the strength of the emotion passing between them. Well, this did not bode well.

"I have pictures to take," I said, and headed out of the line of fire.

I did my photojournalist thing until the parade was about to begin, then I rushed down Main to find a good spot to watch the festivities.

I had pretty much despaired of getting to see anything, since I'm five-two and everybody else was in front of me. Then I heard my name being called.

Steve waved, then motioned for me. We headed to Henry's store, and I followed him upstairs. Like Jake's building, Henry's was two stories. Unlike Jake's, Henry used his upstairs for storage. The big, currently open, window provided a great view of the parade. Margaret was there with Henry's employee. Ronny smiled warmly at me, and I couldn't help but like the young man. Polite, cheerful, exuding energy and charm, I could see why Henry had hired him.

We said our hellos then turned to the parade starting below us. The harsh bellow of sirens announced the police and fire vehicles leading the way. Using the cacophony as a fanfare, the town dignitaries followed in open convertibles. After that came floats pulled behind pickup trucks, the Ugly Creek High School Band, and the former Miss Ugly Creek winners. Maddie and Liza rode together in a decorated convertible, crowns on their heads, waving happily to the adoring crowd. Then came the current Miss Ugly Creek and the two runners-up.

After the beauty queens came the cute kids from the dance school. Tiny bees and fairies danced down the street with older, tuxedo-clad tap dancers, and traditionally dressed ballerinas.

Following behind the dance school cuties was a pickup truck filled with waving children. Some of the kids were bald, some had IV's, and with them were uniformed medical personnel. On the side of the truck was a banner announcing Willow County Children's Hospital. Under that, in much smaller letters, were the words, "Sponsored by Thomas Furniture," and Henry himself was driving the truck.

"The kids love being part of the parade," Margaret said.

I brushed an errant tear from my cheek.

I was still feeling warmth from that when the Blackwood Antiques float pulled into view. I'd seen it earlier from a distance, but I'd stayed away to prevent exactly what happened when I ran into Jake earlier.

Maddie was going to kill me, and I didn't blame her in the least.

Forcing that thought away, I looked back toward the float below. Decorated in red, white, and blue, the flat surface was dotted with chairs holding uniformed veterans, retired police officers, and firemen. Several large pictures graced the middle of the structure, the largest labeled, "Virgil Clark." Overseeing it all was a Statue of Liberty figure.

Instead of the usual pickup, an antique fire truck pulled the float—driven by Jake himself.

Pride filled my heart. Henry and Jake were wonderful men and I was honored to know them both. Margaret was a lucky woman, as was whoever wound up with Jake.

The thought of another woman with Jake tore at me, especially since that woman might well be Maddie. That is, if my harebrained scheme succeeded.

Okay, that was enough of that. I focused my attention back on the parade.

The horses rode through last with a man following behind carrying a huge pooper scooper, apparently insurance in case of an ill-mannered animal.

"I should reopen the store," Ronny said, and took off down the stairs.

Margaret looked around the group, a crafty expression on her face. "It's showtime, folks."

"I'd better get going." Steve turned and headed out the door.

I felt a touch of nausea. Maybe I ate something I shouldn't have. There was some dizziness too, maybe I was getting sick. I put my hands to my cheeks to see if they were hot. Was it too late to call everything off?

"You're doing a good thing, sweetie. It'll be fine."

"Are you sure? Maybe this really isn't such a smart idea. What if it doesn't work?"

Margaret looked deep into my eyes, her expression soft, caring, searching, the kind of expression I would give years of my life to see on my mother. "Do you believe this can work?"

A small, warm surge of belief swirled inside me. "Yes, I do."

Margaret smiled. "Then let's do it."

She headed downstairs, and I was right behind her.

Margaret stayed in Henry's store to prepare for Victim One. I went in search of Liza, who Steve swore was happy to help, and Maddie, AKA Victim Two.

I met Liza and Maddie walking toward me from the direction of an old abandoned gas station—the designated end-of-parade location. Liza indicated the formal gown she still wore. "We're using Henry's store to change."

Maddie only glared.

Liza gave me a reassuring smile as we walked together down the street. Maddie stayed completely quiet, her glare focused on the sidewalk. I walked next to Liza and prayed my crazy scheme would work. Even if she hated me even more after this, it would be worth it if Maddie and Jake could work out their problems.

If that meant they really were in love, then I'd just have to deal with it. If I could. Thankfully, it was all theory right now. I liked to think of myself as a seriously moral, stand-up kind of gal, but does anybody really know what they'd do in a situation like that?

I hoped I didn't have to find out.

We reached Henry's store, and I heard a thump and muttered cussing.

"What was that?" Maddie asked.

"Henry must have dropped something. On his foot," Liza told her.

Maddie narrowed her eyes. "Henry cusses?"

Liza shrugged. "Only if he's alone in the storeroom and drops something on his toe?"

Maddie wasn't buying it.

"Maybe you should give him a few minutes to get himself together," I said.

"Fine with me." Maddie dumped the duffel bag she was carrying in a corner and dropped onto a small beige couch. "This is comfy. We need one like this for the apartment."

She seemed to realize she'd spoken to me, and turned away.

Steve came from the back into the showroom. His shirt had a button missing, and his hair was seriously mussed. As he walked, he adjusted his glasses. "Hi."

Maddie frowned. "What are you doing here?"

"I stuck around after the parade to help Henry with a project."

For a geek, Steve wasn't a bad liar. Then again, that statement was almost true.

"We heard Henry back there," Liza said. "Did he hurt his toe or something?"

His wife, on the other hand was terrible. I could see Maddie's expression out of the corner of my eye. She was quickly becoming suspicious. Not good. I forced a chuckle. "I was amazed to hear cuss words come out of his mouth."

Huh-oh. I'm a decent liar, but Maddie and I spend a lot of time together. She knows me too well. The look she gave me said things were unraveling rapidly. Crap.

"Ouch!"

"That's my mom's voice." Maddie leapt to her feet and before any of us could react, she'd taken off toward the back. Liza, Steve, and I headed after her, trying to get through the door at the same time and bouncing off each other like the Three Stooges as we went.

I shoved into the backroom to see Maddie standing in the middle of the floor, eyes huge, mouth open, staring at Jake tied up in a chair. Henry and Margaret stood near him, both of them looking rather worse for the wear.

"Are you all right, Mom?" Maddie asked.

Margaret smiled. "I'm fine, sweetheart."

Maddie turned a glare on Jake. "What did you do to my mother?"

Jake sent a narrow-eyed, fire-starting glare toward her. Through the duct tape over his mouth came muffled four-letter words. Well, now we knew who'd been cussing.

I felt more than saw Liza streak by me and tackle Maddie. She had her on the floor before I realized what was happening. "I could use some help here," Liza said, raising her cast enough to remind us she was injured. We immediately leapt into action.

It took some doing to get Maddie up and into the chair. Tying her in took everything we had. At one point, a stiletto flew by my head, barely missing. "Watch out," I said. "She's still got her high heels on."

Margaret grabbed one shoe and then the other, giving her daughter an I-dare-you look as she did. Behind Maddie, Steve was tying her arms. Liza had slapped a piece of duct tape across Maddie's #6 Sun Kissed Peach lipsticked mouth. From behind the tape came words I'd never heard Maddie say. This better work, or I was in really deep do-do.

It was then I realized everybody had stepped back and were looking at me. It was time.

I bravely, or maybe foolishly, stood between the kidnapped adversaries. "I know you're both pretty angry right now, and I don't blame you. I'm not totally clear about what happened ten years ago, and what the fire had to do with why you two seem to want to kill each other. The one thing I am sure of is what you feel isn't hate, it's caring. From what I've seen, your biggest problem is neither of you will come within twenty feet of the other. How can you work out your problems if you won't talk?"

I took a deep breath and ignored four eyes shooting resentment and fury my way. "Now you *have* to talk. You don't have a choice. We're going to leave you alone and let you work it out." I pulled the duct tape off their mouths and turned to leave.

For a moment it was quiet, too quiet. At the door I turned back to see Maddie and Jake glaring hard at each other. I took a long, deep breath and prayed I was doing the right thing.

I closed the door behind me and walked over to where the rest of the kidnapping cohorts were gazing anxiously toward the back room door. "It'll work," I told them, though I was not at all sure it would.

We trooped over to the nearest living room display and sat waiting. My stomach was doing gold medal gymnastics and my throat was so dry I don't think water was wet enough to help. And still it was quiet.

Liza crossed one chiffon covered leg over the other, then reversed them. After a couple more of the shifts, she gave up, took off her heels, and pulled her legs underneath her.

I sighed. This was not what I'd pictured when my demented brain came up with this cockamamie plan.

It started as the muffled sound of voices. I held my breath for a moment, then let out a long, relieved sigh. It was in the middle of that sigh that the yelling started. Loud, harsh, and even through the closed door I could make out the dirty words. *Oh crap.*

"They have a lot to get out of their systems," Henry said.

"Ten years' worth," Liza added.

So we sat and sat and waited, and waited and sat.

The bell over the front door dinged and Henry stood. "Better go see about the customer."

I figured he wanted to make sure they stayed away from the back of the store. Good plan, because the yelling was getting louder. My throat was getting raw just listening to them.

There was a crash and we all jumped to our feet. Before we could get anywhere, the back room door swung open with a force that should have taken the hinges off, and Madison stood glaring us down with wide, wild eyes, like the magic-addicted Willow in that Buffy show. Yeah, okay, I watched a few episodes. So sue me.

"I can't believe you did this to me. All of you. My friends. My *mother*! What the hell did you think you were doing?"

"We were trying to help," I said.

"Like when you kissed Jake earlier? I'd hate for my feelings to stand in the way of your new romance." The expression on her face was half angry and half wounded. It tore at me, and I knew for sure I'd be looking for a new roommate.

And a new friend.

She spread her hostility over the group one last time before she stomped out the door.

Liza sat down and let her head sag back onto the couch. "She's going to kill us."

"Probably," Steve said.

"I'm going after her." Margaret took off out the door.

I felt the hair at the back of my head stand up, and I turned to find Jake glaring me down. "I told you to stay out of this."

"I'm sorry," I croaked.

"Yeah, yeah." He stomped out the door.

"I'm going to try to talk some sense into him," Steve said.

"You're a brave man, my husband," Liza said. "Go with God."

Steve rolled his eyes and headed out the door.

I dropped into the nearest chair. Disaster. Total, complete, call-the-governor disaster, that's what I'd caused. Just call me Hurricane Stephie.

"I hate to do this to you," Liza said, "but I really need to get home. We've got family coming over later. You know how it is."

*Not a clue.* "Yeah, pretty stressful."

She leaned her head back and sighed thoroughly. "Ain't that the truth."

My gaze moved toward the front door where two people I cared for deeply had walked out of my life. Probably for good.

"It could still work, you know."

I turned to her, sure I'd heard wrong. "How?"

"They finally talked. Yeah, it was more yelling than talking, but still they communicated. It's going to be harder to ignore each other from now on."

"But Maddie's going back to D.C. in a couple of days." And I'd be looking for a new place to live.

"It's the twenty-first century. Cell phones, email, texting, smoke signals. Plus it's not *that* far down here. It's not like Ugly Creek is on a different plane of existence or something." Liza stood and grabbed her duffle bag from where she'd stashed it. "It'll work out because Maddie and Jake love each other. Need a ride back to Margaret's house?"

All the life dropped out of me. I was still moving around, but I felt dead inside.

A voice that sounded like mine said, "I don't have a key."

She held up the duffle bag Madison had tossed earlier. "I have Maddie's."

We headed out, the bouncy ex-cheerleader and the zombie.

Chapter 15

Three hours later, I was sitting at Margaret's kitchen table, cup of tea in my hand, wondering if I should be packing up and getting out while I still could. Before the person I'd tried to help decided to go all Slayer Buffy on me. Then again, Maddie was my friend. My closest friend. I couldn't just leave her here after the mess I'd made.

The sound of a car pulling in the driveway told me the time for cowardly retreat was past. I'd have to face up to my mistake. I stood and edged around so I could see the front door without being seen.

Maddie blew in and stomped up the stairs. Margaret followed her into the house, her shoulders drooped, her eyes were red, gloom radiated from every cell of her body.

"Are you okay?"

She looked at me, startled. "Stephie. I'm glad you got home all right. I was worried."

"Liza gave me a ride, and she had Maddie's key, I hope that's all right."

The smile was small and shaky. "Of course it is. I should have given you your own key."

I went over to her, my hand going without thought to her arm. "I'm so sorry about all this."

This time her smile was genuine. "You didn't do anything wrong, sweetie. You tried to help."

"And failed miserably."

She brushed an unruly curl off my cheek. "You did what the rest of us have tried and failed at for ten years. You got them talking. Now it's up to them."

Almost the same thing Liza had said. Nice people, these Ugly Creek folks.

Margaret and I walked toward the kitchen. "I made a cup of tea, I hope you don't mind."

"Of course not." She turned the water on to reheat. "Nothing better after a stressful day than a nice cup of tea."

"They really care about each other, don't they?"

"Maddie and Jake? They always did. They were inseparable from the time they were in diapers until ten years ago. They're a good match for each other because they're both so stubborn. But right now stubbornness is what's keeping them apart."

My heart wasn't just breaking; it was slowly tearing into confetti. Jake and Maddie. Maddie and Jake. I felt like dropping my head onto the table and crying my eyes out.

Margaret had just poured her tea when a knock at the front door caught her attention. She headed that way and I edged so I could see. The silly romantic girl inside me dreamed it was Jake come to take me away from all this.

The rest of me wondered, what now?

Henry was on the other side of the door. He pulled Margaret into a kiss, and I went back to my tea. I heard something about Steve and Jake coming to blows, and I wanted to crawl into a hole and never come out.

They came into the kitchen and I managed a smile for Henry. "Thanks for your help," I told him.

"You're very welcome." He grinned. "I haven't had so much excitement since my Uncle Bartholomew threw his back out at one of those lady-of-ill-repute houses. My cousin and I had to go over there and get him out, and it was, shall we say, interesting."

Margaret got him a cup of tea and we all sat at the table. Soon they were engaged in their own conversation and I excused myself and went out onto the screened-in back porch. I loved it out there, where the scorching July heat was brought under control by big trees and a gentle breeze. I could live out there, I decided.

I sat for hours, contemplating how I'd done something so bad to my brother that he'd actually run from me. And now I'd managed to screw up my relationship with my best friend and a man I was feeling pretty strongly about. Not to mention, an unsavory scum was trying, clumsily, to find something in my background distasteful enough to suit his yuckiness. Boy had I screwed up. What a doofus I was.

I saw movement in the growing darkness, and I leaned forward in my seat to see more clearly. It was him, the little furry Bigfoot critter, well, little compared to the other one I'd seen. I smiled and waved, and to my surprise, he waved back.

For a moment it seemed as though he was edging toward the porch, then all at once he turned and scurried back toward the woods.

I sat until almost midnight, waiting for any sign of the cute little creature. There was nothing though, and finally I headed back into the house.

Henry and Margaret were sitting on the living room couch, heads leaned back, and I could hear soft snoring coming from their direction. I smiled, hot date for the middle aged set.

But then, they were no doubt worn out from the events of the day.

Events of my making.

I tiptoed upstairs into the dark bedroom, quietly slipped into my nightshirt, and crawled into bed.

It was hours before I could let go of the guilt enough to sleep.

****

The sound of my cell phone jarred me awake. I groped on the nightstand until I realized I'd left my phone in my purse. I considered getting out of bed to find the thing, but when the annoying sound abruptly stopped, I lay back down and the soft, warm arms of sleep pulled me close.

The phone started up again.

"Answer the damn thing already," Maddie's slurred voice said.

I slid to the foot of the bed, and used my hand to brace myself so I didn't take a header against the softly carpeted floor. I grabbed my purse and shoved myself back on the bed to dig out the phone. By this time the ringing had stopped again and restarted. "Hi," I managed.

"What the bloody hell do you think you're doing?"

I pulled the phone back and stared at it. "Mr. Grainger?"

"Who the hell were you expecting? You're lucky it's me and not our lawyer."

This had to be a bad dream. It just had to be. Nothing else made any sense. I pinched myself, and it hurt. Sunshine was pouring in the window. Okay, now I was totally confused.

"Well, Stephanova, what do you have to say for yourself?"

This had to be a dream. A nightmare. "I'm sorry, Mr. Grainger, I don't know what you're talking about."

"You do understand you're fired. You signed an exclusivity contract with us. *The Weekly Tattler* isn't exactly a competitor, but its national distribution puts you in violation of your contract. If it were up to me, I'd fire you for stupidity. I expected better from you. Get your things out of here ASAP." The line went dead.

I sat staring at the phone and wondering what in the world had just happened. Nothing my boss had said made sense. Had he called the wrong person to chew out? No, not Mr. Grainger. Besides, he'd called me by name. What in the world had I done? I'd been here, in Ugly Creek, how could I have managed to get myself in this much trouble? It had to be a mistake, it just had to be. I headed toward the bathroom. Maybe a gallon of cold water on my face would wake me up—or at least help me figure out what had happened to my world.

The first thing I heard when I stepped back into the bedroom was Maddie's voice. "Thanks for letting me know, Greg."

I walked carefully back toward my bed, wondering when the next wave of weirdness would hit. I didn't have to wait long.

"How could you? I thought I knew you, but you betrayed my trust. That was bad enough, but to betray the entire Ugly Creek community is beyond loathsome."

I stared at her. What was going on here? I shook my head to clear it. Maybe I'd been drugged, or I was in the middle of an especially tenacious dream. I pinched my arm again, but the pain didn't pull me out of the Twilight Zone.

"What do you think I did?"

Maddie didn't answer she just glowered harder than I'd ever thought she could.

"Tell me. What do you think I did?"

She didn't blink. "Don't play games with me, Buffy. I may be from a small town, but I'm not stupid."

Tears filled my eyes, and my throat closed so tightly I could barely speak. "I don't know what you're talking about."

"I don't believe you."

Maddie climbed out of bed and grabbed some clothes. "I'm going to get dressed."

She glared hard at me as she walked out of the room. Alone, I contemplated the scattered pieces of my heart.

I grabbed the only pair of jeans and T-shirt I'd brought and pulled them on with shaking hands. The cool air from the central system chilled me almost as much as the confrontation with Maddie had. I pulled on a light sweater and sat on the edge of the bed.

I had absolutely no idea what was going on. First my boss, then Maddie. And of course she believed the worst of me after I forced her to talk to Jake. I'd only been trying to help, but she wouldn't see it that way. And neither would he. The tears I'd managed to staunch so far filled my eyes. Suddenly I wanted more than anything in this world for Jake to hold me in his arms. I wanted to lean against his rock-hard chest. I wanted to explain to him that I was lost and confused even before I'd agreed to come to Ugly Creek.

Surprise froze me in the process of reaching for the errant tear sliding down my cheek. What a ridiculous idea. I was happy with my life. I had a good job, a nice apartment, a roommate who was closer than a sister.

Except I no longer had any of those things. I wanted Jake so much the agony of it burned me deep inside, a place I didn't know existed, a place I think might be the lonely hole where love should fit.

With a big sigh, I forced myself off the bed and began putting my clothes back in my suitcase. I had to get away from this house. This town. From the craziness that had twisted my life all around since I'd come to Ugly Creek.

From the man I cared way too much about.

"I see you're packing. Good."

For the first time since I'd answered my cell, I felt the burn of anger through my gut and into my chest. "We've been friends since college. We've shared an apartment for three years. How can you possibly believe I'd do whatever it is you think I did?" Then again, she didn't tell me about Bigfoot.

Maddie gave a little one shouldered shrug. "While I was tied up in the back of Henry's store I realized I don't really know you at all."

Tears stung my eyes and I tried to blink them back. "I just wanted to help."

She took a step toward me, and I saw tears cover her eyes. "What's between Jake and me is nobody's business but ours."

"You love each other." I was surprised the words didn't slay me right there.

There was a faraway, beaten expression on her face. "That is none of your business, you traitorous bitch."

"Maddie…"

She rushed toward me and shoved her phone in my face. "Deny that."

What I saw stunned me. The photo was the one I'd taken of the smaller Bigfoot. Worse, it was obvious even on the small screen the picture was on the front page of *The Weekly Tattler*.

She turned and stomped out the door.

I sat hard on the foot of the bed. Never in my life could I have believed I could feel this shocked and devastated. And alone.

I took a moment to allow myself to recover a little, then I did what I'd been doing for most of my life. I pulled myself together and did what I had to do.

I dug my laptop out of the linen closet, grabbed my bag and purse, and carried my stuff downstairs while I wondered what to do next. I could hear voices from the living room and my gaze swung in that direction.

Margaret glared at me through the doorway. "Madison told me what you did."

Behind her, Maddie looked at me with righteous fury.

"I didn't do this, Margaret. You have to believe me."

"I don't have to believe anything, Stephie. I want to believe it's some kind of mistake, but it sure doesn't look like it."

The knock startled me so badly it hurt.

Margaret opened the door, and Henry handed her what I knew was a copy of *The Weekly Tattler*. For a second I hoped the whole, stupid mistake would be revealed and we could all go back to our lives.

"That's my backyard," Margaret said pointing at the tabloid. "That picture was taken in my backyard."

There it was, that morning's issue of the worst tabloid on the supermarket stands, *The Weekly Tattler*. On the front page was my shot of the creature. The headline read, "Award-winning Photographer Up Close and Personal with Bigfoot."

"I didn't do this."

"Your name is on the article." Tears shimmered in Margaret's eyes.

"I didn't."

"Didn't what?" Maddie asked." Didn't take the picture? Because I recognize your style."

*The Weekly Tattler*. Mr. Grainger had mentioned that name. Was this what he was talking about? This picture had violated my contract? It wasn't possible. This was a nightmare. It had to be.

"Well, did you?"

A huge drum was beating against my skull, I had an all but overwhelming urge to throw myself at their feet and beg them to believe me. Somehow, I managed to keep myself in adult mode. "I took the picture, but I didn't send it to the *Tattler*. I'd never do something like that."

"Why should we believe that?" Maddie took a step toward me. "You even gave them an interview."

*What!* My hands were shaking so hard I ripped the tabloid as I grabbed it from Margaret's hands. Sure enough, there was an interview supposedly given by me. "I don't understand."

Maddie walked by me, and I had the sudden thought I might literally be stabbed in the back—not that I much cared. "I didn't do this." I looked from

Henry to Margaret and back again. Margaret's face was pale and I could see she was trembling. Henry was quieter, not meeting my gaze, but not saying anything either. Tears stung my eyes, but hard-learned lessons prevented them from falling.

Maddie came back from the entryway where I'd dropped my things, my laptop case in her hand. "Steve can prove what you did."

"Fine." I wiped at my eyes. "He can do whatever he wants with that." I had to get out of there. I had to go back to my apartment. Maybe, maybe if I got back to D.C. I'd find this was all a horrible nightmare. "Could somebody take me to town so I can rent a car?"

"I will." Henry stood and walked me over to my things. He took my suitcases and turned toward the door.

The etiquette part of my brain screamed at me to say goodbye and thank you to my hostess, but I figured the faster I got out the better. I'd send a card, I promised myself. Maybe a gift.

Maybe she'd send me one. Maybe a bomb.

The drive into town was silent except for my sniffles. I wanted to talk to Henry, but he was the only one who hadn't said anything about what a monster I was, and I really wanted to keep it that way.

He pulled into the rental car lot and I started to get out, but a hand grabbed my wrist and held me in place.

"Did you send the picture to that sorry excuse for a newspaper?"

I looked him right in the eye. "No. I would never do that." Tears blurred my vision. "I like that little furry fellow."

He studied my face for a few long, tense moments,

then slowly nodded. "I believe you."

I felt like I was a balloon and the air had just been let out. I collapsed against the seat. "Thank you."

"Give 'em time to figure things out. Madison's still mad over that craziness yesterday. And Margaret is a momma. Mommas are protective over young ones, even if they aren't hers."

That verified what I'd assumed. "The little creature, it's a child."

Henry nodded. "He's nine, and pretty much equivalent to a human nine-year-old, except for being almost as tall as I am. They don't have many kids, you know."

"No, I didn't know."

"Yeah. Don't know why, but they don't. So we all tend to be kinda protective of the critters, especially the young ones."

"They're amazing."

The sides of his lips twitched in the direction of a smile. "You don't know the half of it."

"Thank you, Henry. For giving me the benefit of the doubt."

He did smile then. "You take care of yourself. I'll be looking forward to seeing you again real soon."

"I don't know about that. I kinda think I wore out my welcome here in Ugly Creek."

He shook his head. "You belong here, Stephie."

I snorted. "Yeah right." Grabbing my stuff, I started toward the front door of the rental company, only to have Henry take the suitcase away from me and carry it inside the building.

"Bob, this is my friend Stephie. You treat her real good now."

"I'll do that, Henry."

Henry honored me with a warm smile and a quick hug before he headed out.

"So, what can I do for you today young lady?" Bob asked.

Twenty minutes later, I was driving a gray Toyota, but instead of heading north like anybody with a lick of sense would do, I was steering down Main Street. I wanted my antique clothing, I told myself. I didn't want to entrust the things to the postal service. I was close; I could just run by and grab the chest.

Okay, I admit it. I wanted to see Jake again. I missed him and I hadn't even left yet.

Since it was Sunday, there was almost no traffic. I parked the car a couple of blocks down the street from the antique shop. There was no sign of anyone home, but I couldn't see where Jake parked his truck, so I couldn't say for sure. I just sat for a minute. My heart ached to go in. but I knew I couldn't.

Then I saw Jake and Dingo trot up the street. Man and dog, running and playful. My eyes filled at the sight. Every molecule inside me wanted to get out of the car and head straight for them.

I loved him.

The thought thrust itself into my chest with the power of an EF-five tornado. Great. Within the space of one, bright Sunday morning I'd been fired, accused of betraying my best friend, her mother—who I'd come to see as a substitute mother—a truly cool group of creatures, and apparently an entire town. Nobody was listening except one odd man. And now the disaster was complete. I was in love with a guy I was pretty sure was my closest friend's soulmate.

I put the car in gear and drove out of sight of the store. On a deserted side street, I sat and contemplated my choices. There was no way in hell for this situation to end well. If by some miracle Jake believed I hadn't sent the picture, if Maddie realized I didn't do it, if every person in town believed I had done nothing to deserve their hatred; even then I'd have to go. There's no way I could take the man she loved away from Maddie, I could never do something like that to a woman I loved like a sister.

Best case scenario, Jake hated my guts. If so, my beaten and bruised heart couldn't stand to hear what he had to say.

Yep, it was better all around if I just went back to D.C., packed my stuff, and headed off somewhere to start a new life.

This time, I couldn't hold back the tears. I wiped at my eyes, forced myself to buck up, and pulled out onto the road.

Just past the business district, I lowered my window. The breeze wasn't exactly cool, but it carried the fresh scent of cut grass and summer sun. I not only loved Jake, I loved this town. What I wanted more than anything was to start again right here, in Ugly Creek, Tennessee. Listen to your heart, Aunt Octavia had said, and I really, really wished I could.

What my heart cried out for was impossible, of course, but logic did nothing to lessen the longing.

There went the tears again. Good grief! I was turning into the River of Denial. I may be a little dense at times, but I'm not stupid, I did eventually figure out I couldn't drive with my vision blurry and my mind filled with wadded-up bits of confusion, worry, and longing for things I could never have.

I pulled over at a widened area with two picnic tables and a coppery sign with black lettered information about the history of Ugly Creek—the actual creek, not the town. In spite of everything, I was curious. I couldn't read it with my eyes so blurry, though, so I ignored the sign for the moment and promised myself I'd take a picture of it on my way out. Dragging my reluctant body over to the closest concrete picnic table, I sat on an attached bench and dropped my head into my hands.

Being alone wasn't exactly a new thing in my life, but it was the first time I hadn't had a plan. I was lost, unprepared, scared. What was I supposed to do now?

Probably because I was having a pity party, I almost didn't realize I was no longer alone. A rustling in the bushes alerted me to a presence and I prayed it wasn't a murderer come to convince me to be his next victim.

It might not take much convincing given the state I was in.

What I saw shocked me more than a murderer would have. It was the young Bigfoot creature, the subject of the photo that had stolen my world and flung it back at me.

I smiled and waved at him, hoping he wasn't there to take revenge for the wrong everyone thought I'd done. Though who could blame him?

When he began to walk toward me, I stood and backed away to give me more time. This might be a child, but he was as tall as a grown man. "I didn't send that photo to *The Weekly Tattler*, honest."

He leaned his head to one side a very human, very

214

confused expression pulled at his face. "Help. Please."

The creature's odd, low-pitched voice was reminiscent of the larger creature's but it was obvious this little guy was very unsure of his English. And me too, probably.

"Help?" I asked. "Do you want to help me or do you need help?"

"Need," he said. "Bad man. Father hurt. Please help." He pointed toward the direction from which he'd come. "There."

"Let's go."

I trucked off behind the furry kid, and discovered the varmint could run like a cross-country track champion. Before long, he had to stop and wait on his short-legged human companion. Between trying to breathe and wondering if I was having a heart attack, I thought about what I was rushing headlong into. Bad man. Father hurt. Just what was it I thought I could do to help?

I realized the kid had stopped and was holding one furry finger up to his mouth. Quiet? Oh boy.

I slowed and crept toward him as quietly as I could, wondering if my gasping breath and pounding heart wasn't clearly audible to anyone in a one mile radius.

When I got to him, he pulled me behind a bush and pointed.

By this time, I could hear a voice, a voice I recognized. Butch. Great. That's all I needed to make this day a complete and glorious disaster.

I peeped over the bush and saw him holding a gun on a huge Bigfoot that looked to be the same one Butch had argued with at the picnic, and the big guy was bleeding from one shoulder. I swallowed hard. The furry dude was massive, almost as tall as several of the smaller trees. Butch must be crazier than I thought.

Movement pulled my gaze from the Bigfoot, and I saw someone standing beside them. Brandon.

I couldn't help it; I gasped and almost lost my footing. Instinctually, I grabbed the foliage to keep from falling on my butt. The noise I made was unmistakable in the quiet forest area.

Butch looked at me and grinned. "Well, well, well, look who's here. Come on and join the party."

"Help get," the furry kid whispered and vanished without a sound into the trees.

I walked toward Butch, my hands held up so he could see them. "Butch, what are you doing out here?"

He cut his eyes toward the Bigfoot. "I'm trying to talk this coward into taking responsibility for what he did."

"I have told you many times. I did not cause the fire."

"The fire at the gym?" I guessed.

"Yeah, the one I took the blame for," Butch said.

"I thought the fire was ruled an accident," I said.

Butch snorted. "Officially, but everybody in town believes I started it. I'm tired of being the black sheep of Ugly Creek."

I could relate to that. "Let's all go back to town and sit down and talk about this."

"Hell no!" Butch waved the gun so fiercely I was afraid it would accidentally go off. "I ain't going to talk to nobody until this varmint here is ready to admit what he did."

"You don't need Buffy, why don't you let her go?"

I looked at my brother with surprise. His gaze was

locked on Butch, but I caught a glimpse of fear on his face. I wasn't clear on what this was all about, but it was more than just an attempt to clear Butch's name. Whatever was going on, my baby brother was in way over his head.

Butch grinned toward me. "Buffy and me got some things to talk about."

"Nope," I told him. "We most definitely don't."

"Let her go, Butch. We can make the Sasquatch talk."

Butch shoved the gun into the creature's side. "If I could have got Nootau's kid he'd have admitted what he did by now. But I managed to hook up with incompetent help." He leveled a look of sheer hatred toward my brother.

Brandon took a step toward Butch, and I must have had one of those psychic visions or something, because I knew the kid was about to put himself in danger. "Let my sister go, Johnson."

"Maybe Bigfoot...Nootau...is telling the truth," I said.

Butch snorted. "He ain't. I know he snuck around back behind the gym and smoked sometimes. Me and the other boys gave him cigarettes. I know damn well I put out my light. When I left he was still standing there."

"I did not smoke that night. I did not cause the fire," Nootau said.

Out of the corner of my eye, I saw Brandon edge toward Butch. Butch must have seen him too, because he turned toward my brother and growled.

"Let Brandon go," I said.

"He's helping me," Butch said. "Aren't you, boy?"

"I will, if you let my sister go."

Butch rolled his eyes. "Well, aren't we the sweet little family?"

"Put the gun down, Johnson."

The familiar voice came from the trees on the left. Jake stepped into the clearing, and I swallowed back tears of relief. Near where Jake stood, I caught a glimpse of the small creature barely visible in the foliage.

Butch snorted. "And just why would I want to do that?"

"Because the police are on their way."

"Good, because somebody wants to make a confession." Butch poked the Bigfoot with the gun.

"I did not start the fire."

"Well, if you don't care about yourself, maybe you care about somebody else."

Before I knew what was happening, Butch grabbed me and pulled me against him, my back to his chest, his arm around my waist, the gun pressed to the side of my head. "How about you admit what you did so she stays alive?"

"Don't hurt my sister!" Brandon rushed over. "Please!"

Butch grinned. "I didn't think you cared about *Buffy* here."

I hated the way he made my name sound like a cuss word. Through gritted teeth I said, "Ms. Stephanova to you, jerk!"

"Let her go, Butch," Jake said, edging closer.

"I should have known you'd come running to save her. She didn't want me. Just like all the others. Didn't want anything to do with me but ran to you. Even though you and her 'best friend' apparently want to kill each other." With his chin he indicated the Bigfoot. "Courtesy of the fire he started."

"All right," Bigfoot said. "I will admit responsibility for the fire. Now please let the woman go."

"As soon as you admit what you did to the authorities." Butch leaned over my shoulder and licked my cheek. I was barely able to fight back the gag reflex. "Then you and me can talk," he whispered.

When hell froze over, I thought, but didn't think saying it would get me anywhere. My mind swirled and swam in an attempt to figure a way out of the situation.

"I'm sorry, Buffy."

I looked into Brandon's eyes and saw love.

"I'm going to get you out of this," Jake's voice came from behind me.

The foliage rustled, and I saw Maddie, Liza, and Steve standing close, apparently waiting for a chance to save me. And there was love in Maddie's eyes. In spite of everything that had gone so utterly wrong, she was willing to put her life in danger for me.

This place was quickly becoming Grand Central Ugly Creek. If Butch lost it, there could be a lot of carnage.

*You and those you love*, Aunt Octavia had said. *Betrayal and peril*. Something about my choice and the outcome. Dang, I need to write this vision stuff down.

"I'll bet Washington would be an interesting place to live," Butch said.

"It's great," I said. "Lots of parties and stuff. And everybody is rich." I told you I was a pretty decent liar.

"We could go there together," he said. "You could

show me around." He fondled my hair, and I wanted badly to fondle him with my fist.

"I could be rich." He was staring off into his bright future, but I was listening to something a little closer to home. I knew that sound all too well, and my gaze moved to a pile of rocks about five feet to the side of dumbass and me. Great, just what we needed to make this party complete.

Brandon took a step toward us, and I shook my head. "Don't do it, kid." He frowned and was about to ignore me. I had to do something quick. "Do you remember that summer we played in the Qualls' shed? The one with all the tires?"

His eyes widened, and I knew he remembered. I used my chin to gesture toward the rock pile. His face abruptly paled and he backed away.

Butch laughed. "Good little boy. Always does what his sister tells him to."

"Only when she's right," Brandon said.

I realized Bigfoot…um…Nootau was slowly edging toward the rocks. I managed to catch his gaze and shake my head. To my surprise, he smiled and winked. Something told me he knew what was lurking under there. What in the world was he up to?

"Stop moving around," Butch told Bigfoot.

The movement stopped, and Butch turned his attention back to me. "Tell me some more about how great it is in Washington."

"Lots of money to be made," I lied. "You're a smart guy. There are buckets of opportunities for somebody like you."

I looked over my shoulder at him and used up about ninety percent of the energy I had left to smile into his revolting face.

I could almost see visions of assets swirling in his brain, while behind him, Big Hairy Guy edged toward the rocks. Cold sweat popped out on my forehead. If he was going to do anything at all like I suspected he might, things were about to go from bad to put-your-head-between-your-legs-and-pray mode.

Just as Nootau reached the rocks, there was a loud rattle. I felt Butch stiffen just before I saw Nootau reach toward the rocks. I held my breath while I hoped to hell he wasn't doing what I thought he was.

He was.

The snake was almost as long as Bigfoot was tall, Nootau held it with both hands, one behind the head and one down the body. At the end of the tail, the sound of rattling came from the mass of scales that gave the rattlesnake its name.

Raising it over his head, Nootau made as if to toss the animal toward Butch—and me.

Butch squealed like a pig, threw me aside, and hurled himself away from the Bigfoot and the snake. I saw Jake grab for me, but he was too far back. For a swine, Butch shoved hard. I bounced off a tree trunk on my way down, and for a moment, everything went black.

When my eyes opened, I saw Jake's handsome face looking down at me. "Are you all right, sweetheart?"

I almost passed out again, from the sheer wonder of him being there, holding me, saying *sweetheart*. Oh my. "I'm okay," I managed.

The sound of scuffling caught my attention, and I turned to see Brandon punching the daylights out of Butch. Steve and Liza were working to stop him, but not with much enthusiasm.

Finally, Steve grabbed Brandon around the waist and set him on his feet out of reach of the cowering Butch. Brandon struggled for a moment longer, then went limp.

His gaze moved toward me and the shadow of agony darkened his face. "Buffy," he groaned, and shook off Steve's grip.

When he dropped beside me, I looked up into the faces of the two people I loved most in the world. For one, totally blissful moment, the world was bright and sweet and birds sang in the trees.

I moved to sit up, only to be pressed back toward the ground. "Lie still."

"I'm okay," I told Jake.

"No, you aren't," Brandon said.

"I was so scared," Jake whispered, and I heard tears in his voice. "I was afraid I was going to lose you."

"Me too." I looked at my little brother, and tears were forming in his eyes. "I'm so sorry, Buff…Stephie."

My heart shattered into dust. "I shouldn't have left you with that monster," I said, surprised a tongue as dry as mine could even work.

"You went away to college; you couldn't take me." There was still a touch of bitterness in his voice, but I saw honesty in his eyes.

"We need to get you to a doctor," Jake said.

"I'm fine," I told him, and tried again to sit up.

Again, a firm hand held me down. "Lay still, sweetheart. You're hurt." And there it was, that look, the one I'd dreamed about, the expression of sheer, pure, amazing love. I was in heaven.

"How bad is she hurt?" Maddie's face appeared, next to Jake's.

And the world came crashing down on me.

I shoved at him. "No," it was all I could manage.

"No? What are you talking about?"

"It can't work between us." My heartbeat stuttered, my heart cried out in agony, then curled up in a ball and lay weeping.

"I know there are things we have to work out." Jake's eyes glistened with welling tears. His voice shook as he continued. "I know your life is in D.C. I'd never ask you to give that up. I'll go to D.C. with you. I'll go to Mars with you. Just please don't leave me."

I couldn't do this. I was a good person and all, but giving up the man I loved—and hurting him in the process—was just more than any human woman could endure. I loved Maddie, and I wanted the best for her, but the ugly truth was I wasn't strong enough to do what I needed to do. I opened my big mouth to tell this awesome man just what kind of feelings he'd provoked inside me.

Then I caught a glimpse of Maddie behind him. "I can't," I said, and the words cut through me like long, sharp icicles. "You love Maddie and she loves you."

"What are you talking about?"

I looked into the eyes of the man I loved more than life itself and knew he'd eventually resent—or even hate—me if I let this happen. It just might kill me to give him up, but I really had no choice.

So I handed him to my best friend. "The two of you belong together. You'll work it out. Just be happy." I glanced toward Maddie. "Both of you."

The sound of a groan caught my attention and I looked to see Liza standing over Butch with a big stick held up like a softball bat. "Don't even think about it, big boy," she told him. Even with a cast on one arm, she was an imposing sight.

His eyes widened to saucer size, and he lay back down.

The sound of Maddie's laughter confused me more than my aching head could tolerate. I looked her way, wondering what in the world she could possibly think was amusing.

"You think Jake and I are…?" Maddie doubled over with hard, explosive laughter, then straightened up and wiped at her eyes. "Do you hear that Jake? She thinks we're a couple."

"A *what*?" he looked totally, completely, utterly, discombobulated.

"You love each other," I managed, utterly amazed I could talk with my heart shredding into pieces and swirling away with the wind.

"Do you love Brandon?" Maddie asked.

I stared at her. What did that have to do with the price of pot roast in Outer Mongolia? "Of course I do."

"And I love Jake." she punched him on the arm.

"Ouch!" He put his hand over where she'd nailed him.

"I love him like a brother." I saw her swallow. "And I couldn't stand to watch my brother suffer so soon after Dad—" She looked at the ground.

"That's why you left while I was still in the hospital?" Jake asked. His face had the haggard expression of one who had experienced deep, all-encompassing agony.

She looked at him, and tears began to slide down her cheeks. "I'm sorry. Mom was so broken up. You just lay there and moaned in pain, and they weren't sure you were going to make it and I just couldn't take it. I couldn't stand to watch my family suffer. I'm a coward, I know. I just couldn't stand to be in Ugly Creek any longer."

Jake stood and pulled her into his arms. "I should have realized that. I'm an idiot."

"Well, I knew that a long time ago," Maddie said, and then dissolved into loud, messy sobs. Yeah, I admit it; it was good to know the always-together Madison Clark could cry messy. On the other hand, it hurt to realize she was that upset. My poor best friend. She'd been hurt more than any of us had realized.

I used the distraction to sit up off the hard dirt. Maybe Maddie wasn't the only coward in the bunch. I looked toward my handsome, six-foot-something-or-other, little brother. "I love you, Brandon. Let's please talk things out."

My bigger-than-me little brother pulled me close and kissed my cheek. "I'd really like that, sis."

"Okay, where's the emergency?"

I turned to see a somewhat overweight, gasping man in a sheriff's uniform coming toward us, the young Bigfoot creature leading the way.

"About time you got here," Liza said. "Fortunately, we have everything under control."

The man eyed Liza and her big stick. "Looks that way."

"Just take that jerk Johnson out of here and lock him up," Jake said, "before one of us decides to take our frustrations out on him."

225

"And we got lots of frustrations," Liza said, narrowing her eyes at the man sprawled at her feet.

The sheriff went over to Butch and shoved him over on his stomach, pulling his arms back in the process.

"I didn't do it," Butch protested.

"You got a truckload of witnesses that say you did."

"Not that. The fire, I didn't start the fire. Nootau did. He admitted it."

"I did not start the gymnasium fire," Nootau said.

The sheriff sighed. "Well, one of you did. We just couldn't prove which one."

"Neither one of them did."

We all looked toward Steve, who, I now realized, hadn't spoken since he'd arrived with Liza and Maddie.

"I started the fire," Steve said. "Or at least I think I did."

I heard Liza's gasp behind me.

"It was an accident," Steve's voice broke, and he swallowed audibly before he continued. "Liza and I had an argument and I was feeling all nervous and antsy. I knew guys smoked behind the gym. I went back there to bum a cigarette from somebody. I thought it'd calm me down." He looked away for a moment while he wiped at his face. "Nobody was there, but I found a butt that was nice and long. I lit it and sucked in a long breath. I thought I was going to die. I coughed and coughed and coughed until I threw up. I was so embarrassed I took off into the woods until I got myself together. Just a few minutes after I got back, the fire alarm went off. It wasn't until later I realized I hadn't put out that damn cigarette. I honestly don't know what happened to it."

"You let me be blamed for all these years!" Butch jerked loose from the sheriff. Bigfoot easily caught him and handed him back to the cop.

"Actually I always figured Nootau was responsible," the sheriff said, "but we weren't sure. When rumors started that Butch started the fire I had no proof either way. The DA couldn't exactly charge Nootau, and for all we knew, Johnson could be the one who did it."

"What are you going to do with my husband?" Liza was pale, and I could see her trembling.

"That's up to the judge," the sheriff said. "But I wouldn't worry too much." He looked toward Steve. "We don't even know for sure you did start that fire. Even if you did, it was an accident. You're a good man, Zapata. I kinda think keeping quiet for all these years was probably more punishment than anything the justice system could do to you."

"His keeping quiet hurt me," Butch protested in a whiny voice even a five-year-old would be embarrassed to use.

"So file a lawsuit." The sheriff snagged Butch and headed toward the road.

Nootau took the snake into the woods, and both Bigfoot creatures headed off toward the mountain.

Liza ran to Steve and they grabbed each other.

I felt an arm around me and realized I was feeling kinda shaky and weak and my head was pounding. "Take it easy," Brandon said. "You got hit pretty hard."

I touched the side of my head and felt a rapidly growing lump under my hair. Great.

"I've got her." Arms lifted me and I looked up into

dark, worried eyes. "I'm okay, Jake," I whispered.

"She needs a doctor," Brandon said.

"I agree," Jake started back toward the road with me in his arms.

I tried to argue, but my heart wasn't in it. Doing a woodsy remake of *An Officer and a Gentleman* with Jake felt just too amazing. Besides, I pretty much had no stuffing left. In the century since I woke up that morning, entirely too many things had happened. Confused, relieved, hopeful, and terrified; I leaned against Jake's strong, firm chest and closed my eyes. I felt safe and happy. That couldn't last though, I knew. There was a mountain of problems still to be dealt with. I could still lose it all.

Chapter 16

Less than thirty minutes later, I lay sprawled on a narrow emergency room stretcher staring at the tiny room across the hall from mine. The curtain was pulled almost completely around the other stretcher, but through a tiny opening, I clearly saw an elbow. An elbow covered with thick, brown fur. There was the sound of a voice, and I recognized the deep rumble of a Bigfoot creature. I was blown away, but it only took a moment for me to reconsider. Where else would they go for medical care, a veterinarian? I actually giggled at the thought of the proud, awesome critters going to a vet. They were definitely more human than dog or cat. Fur notwithstanding.

About that time, a young, good looking male type doctor walked into my room. He followed my gaze across the hall, muttered something I didn't quite catch to the nurse, then stepped into my room. I'm quite sure it was no accident he stood directly in my line of sight. Nor was it an accident the curtain and sliding glass door across the hall both abruptly closed. The nurse joined the doctor in my closet-sized room, and they both stood there looking at me as if I was Hitler's right hand girl. I started to tell them I didn't send that picture to the *The Weekly Tattler*, but I knew that would be a crazy waste of time not to mention probably a bad idea. Better that I not antagonize the nice people with mysterious machines and big needles.

"I'm Doctor Addams," the doctor said. And yes, the name on the badge had two D's in it. "So you bumped your head?"

"No, actually, I got knocked down, hard." I touched, the egg-sized lump on one side of my head, and winced. The area was extremely tender.

Maybe I'm paranoid, but his expression seemed to be one of deep respect—for whoever hit me. "This was an assault?"

"Actually, more of an accident as the result of an assault."

His eyebrows pulled down in confusion. "Was the sheriff notified?'

"Yes," I told him, wishing I'd have just claimed clumsiness.

"Okay then, let's check you out."

I wanted to scream out the rest of the story, but I knew they didn't care and probably wouldn't believe me anyway.

Two hours later, I rolled into the lobby in a wheelchair pushed by one of the medical professionals I now had enormous respect for. In spite of how they apparently felt about me, their treatment was a shining example of caring professionalism.

Jake was sitting in the lobby. He stood when he saw me and rushed my way. "Are you all right?"

"I'm fine," I told him.

He glanced toward the nurse and she confirmed my words. "She needs to rest, Jake, but there's no sign of a concussion." She handed him a sheet of paper. "But it doesn't hurt to watch out for the symptoms anyway and get her back here if anything changes."

"I'll take care of her."

The cute little redheaded nurse nodded, then turned back toward the door we'd come through.

"You know her?" I asked, and there was no jealousy in my voice. Really, there wasn't.

Jake grinned. "I love it when you're jealous. I went to school with her and her husband."

"Oh, okay." I bit my lower lip to hide the smile.

"Let's get you out of here. Dingo's anxious to see you."

A frightening thought hit me so hard I gasped. "You don't know, do you? About the...the picture?"

"The one in that sorry excuse for a newspaper?"

I nodded, worry filling my throat so I couldn't speak and could barely breathe.

Jake sat on his heels in front of my wheelchair and took my hand in his. "I don't know whose bright idea that was, but it wasn't yours."

I stared at him; love for him filled my heart and leaked out my eyes in the form of tears. "You believe in me?"

"Of course I do," he whispered, and pulled me into his arms.

I leaned against his firm chest and fought hard to hold back the sobs. It had been a hellacious day, okay?

"Let's get you home." He helped me to my feet and snuggled me close against him as we walked out to his truck.

He buckled me in, slid behind the wheel, and took off down the road. I leaned against the back of the seat and closed my eyes. He believed in me. Holy alternate universe, the man believed in me. How crazy was that?

I felt him take my hand in his and I turned to smile

his way. I was absolutely convinced the dream was going to end at any moment, but by George, I was going to enjoy it while it lasted.

A few minutes later, Jake wrapped an arm around me and all but lifted me up the stairs to his apartment. As soon as I walked through the door, a little voice inside me whispered, *Home*. That's what it felt like too, warm, safe, comfortable. Home, that mythical place I'd never really known.

Even after we were inside the living room, Jake kept his arm around me. "I'm fine," I told him.

"You were held at gunpoint, thrown against a tree, and knocked on your ass. Fine is one thing you aren't."

I barely managed to hold back the grin. "Bigfoot was held at gunpoint, how come you aren't babying him?"

"One, he didn't hit his head or get knocked on his big ass." He shoved me toward the bedroom, and I got hopeful. "Two, I'm not in love with Bigfoot. Nootau is his wife's problem."

"You love me?" Yeah, I'd seen it in his face, but still a little voice inside kept saying I was mistaken.

He looked deep into my eyes, his hand gently lifting my chin. "More than I've ever loved anyone in my life."

And there it was, the dream of a lifetime, the moment from my fantasies, the moment I never for one moment thought would ever come true. "I love you too," I whispered, as blissful tears filled my eyes.

He edged me down, covered me with a blanket, and sat on the edge of the bed. My hope did a nosedive.

"I'm really okay, you know. The doctor said I'm fine."

"The doctor said you need to rest, so you're going to rest."

"I thought guys only had one thing on their minds."

Jake chuckled. "I do. I only want to make sure the love of my life, the woman I want to spend the rest of time with, is taken care of."

My breath turned thick and refused to move out of my lungs. "What?" I croaked.

He slid into bed beside me, pulled me into his arms and tenderly kissed the top of my head. "You are the most special woman I've ever met. You turned my world upside down and made me believe in forever after, my sweet Stephie." He took my hand in his. "I realize we haven't known each other long, and we have a million things to work through, but I can't imagine life without you."

I put my free fingers against his wide, sexy mouth. "Don't."

"Scared?"

"Hell, yes."

He actually laughed, the rat. "So you'll go up against a guy with a gun, but the very idea of commitment has you running for cover?"

I gave him my very best indignant glare. "I'm not afraid of commitment."

"Oh really?" One side of his mouth twitched in the direction of a smile.

"Really." I tried to put every bit of strength I had into the lie—I mean the word.

"Then you won't mind if I spend some serious time in D.C. trying to convince you we belong together."

"What about your shop?" Yes, I was dodging the question.

"Margaret is perfectly capable of taking care of my store."

My fingers, drawn to his face by the force of desire, touched his cheek and slid downward to his awesome mouth. The darkness in his eyes, and his quick intake of breath had me getting hopeful again.

"You need to rest," he whispered.

"I need *you*." I touched my lips to his in an effort to show him just how much I needed him. The boy was smart. In seconds he had his hands under my clothes and was exploring the topography of my body. A few, heart-pounding minutes later we were both naked.

And then the real fun began.

\*\*\*\*

I sat at Jake's kitchen table that afternoon, munching on scrambled eggs, toast, and crisp bacon. The view across the table was amazing. Tall, handsome, shirtless man, hair wet from his shower, eyes dark and warm; smile wide, gorgeous, and just for me. The warm scent of soap and freshly washed man drifted across the table and did interesting things to the private areas of my body.

I wanted badly to forget everything else and focus on the present. I wanted to pretend we could do this every morning for the rest of our lives. I wanted to not have the conversation we were about to have. But as Mick Jagger says, "You can't always get what you want."

"Jake, we need to talk."

I heard him suck in his breath, then lower his fork. "Damn, those words are never good."

"Just because you believe I didn't send that picture to *The Weekly Tattler*, most of the rest of the world thinks I'm a traitor to Bigfoot kind."

Jake took my hand in his, a serious expression pulling at his forehead and shadowing his eyes. "You have to understand, we've fought for over a hundred years to prevent the Bigfoot clan from being discovered. With every generation, their numbers grow smaller and the population of Ugly Creek gets bigger. The more people who know, the more likely exactly what happened will happen. It's not your fault."

I looked hard at my plate. "I took the picture."

"You didn't send it out."

"No, but I gave whoever did the opportunity." I sighed.

"On your personal computer, right? It's not like you had the photo out waving it around."

I slowly shook my head, thinking. "Nobody but me knew it was even in there, and I don't understand how anybody could have gotten hold of it. I haven't been online since I took the picture, and my computer is password-protected. Plus, I put that shot in a locked file with some of the other Ugly Creek shots. Just landscape stuff, nothing important. I lock my picture files, and the file name was 'Landscape' or something equally earth-shattering."

"Margaret said there was a possible break-in at her house."

"Why would anyone get into my computer instead of just taking it? And if they did, why look in *that* file? I can't believe they went through every picture in my computer; that could take days."

"None of this makes sense."

I leaned back and rubbed my aching head. "That's for sure."

Cheryel Hutton

Jake shook his head. "I think when we figure that out a lot of things will make sense." He glanced at his watch. "We should probably start getting things together, the tribute dinner is at seven o'clock, and I know from long, annoying experience with my sister it takes a while for a woman to get ready."

An icy hand gripped my heart and I felt the blood drain from my face. "I can't go to the dinner."

"Why not?"

I looked into his kind eyes and tried to let him see the agony tearing me apart. "My being there would only upset Maddie. I came here to help her, to make things easier. I can't do something that would make her unhappy."

Jake licked his lips absently, then tilted his head to one side and narrowed his eyes. "Do you trust me?"

"Yes. I do."

"Then trust me enough to allow me to escort you to the dinner."

Even though warning sirens screamed in my head, I did trust him, but there was a problem that might just get me out of the situation. I hoped. "All my clothes are in the rental car. I have nothing to wear."

"Your things are here."

How did that happen? Surprise, and a touch of anxiety, tingled up my spine. "How in the world did you do that? Magic?"

He grinned. "I have my ways. Now let's get going. I don't want to be late."

I wanted to be late. Maybe a week late. Actually, a month would be even better. "Promise me if it gets ugly you'll bring me back here."

"I promise." He pulled me to my feet and hugged

me close. "And there will be no ugly."

I didn't believe him, but I'd blundered through this far, why not take my humiliation all the way. After all, this was Ugly Creek, after all. Why not give the place an opportunity to live up to its name?

At my expense.

Chapter 17

The sun edged the top of the mountain as I stood in the doorway of Ugly Creek High School's gymnasium. I gripped Jake's hand so hard I was sure I was hurting him. He didn't let on though, just smiled reassuringly my way every couple of minutes.

Several people glanced toward me, and some stared. I knew I wasn't welcome, but it was probably too late to back out now.

"I shouldn't be here," I whispered.

"Nonsense," Jake whispered back.

Against my better judgment, I walked with him across the blue tarp protecting the floor toward the maze of tables covered with white tablecloths. At the back of the space, the stage was again set up.

I had no business being here. This was the night to honor Virgil Clark. This was a time for his friends and family. I'd never even met the man. Then there was the little problem that his family, along with most of the people here tonight, hated my guts.

I'd thought I was nervous last time I'd entered this room, just a few days ago, but that was basket weaving. This was calculus, and I suck at calculus.

"It'll be okay," Jake whispered, wrapping his arm around me.

Sure. Any time now those folks over there giving me the death stare will become my very best friends.

Speaking of best friends, I suddenly realized we were headed straight to a table filled with people I was quite sure didn't want to see me.

"Jake," I whispered, "maybe this isn't such a good idea."

"Trust me."

Well hell, I was here, I might as well make a complete fool out of myself. So, with legs of wet French fries, trembling so hard I was beginning to believe we were having an earthquake, I pasted something between a smile and a grimace on my face, and walked toward my doom.

When I got close to the table, I saw Maddie turn and look my way. Oh boy.

She was on her feet and rushing toward me. Did she have a weapon in her hand?

"I'm so sorry!" she said as she grabbed me and hugged so tightly I struggled to breathe.

I felt my legs give out completely and I would have sat in the floor if it weren't for Maddie holding me up.

"You don't hate me?" I whispered.

Maddie's blue eyes filled with tears as she held my gaze. "Absolutely not! I love you. I let my fear and insecurity get ahead of my good sense." She turned her gaze to Jake. "And I damn near lost both of my best friends. Will you ever forgive me?" She looked back and forth between us.

"Of course we will," Jake said. I nodded my agreement since my throat was too clogged with thankfulness to speak.

"I hope you'll extend that forgiveness to me," Margaret said.

I turned to her and saw her red-rimmed eyes.

"I did exactly what I hate other people doing, I judged you harshly without knowing the whole story."

I squeezed Maddie once before I took my shaky legs over to hug Margaret. "I know how it looked. I don't blame you for believing your own eyes."

She hugged me, then glanced behind me as she spoke. "You're a lucky man, Jake. You'd better hold on to this woman."

"I plan to."

"The whole town hates me," I told her.

She shrugged. "Minor problem."

I heard my bitter laugh and cringed. She gently kissed my cheek and shoved me into a chair. Jake took up residence in the next one. Maddie sat next to him, beside her was Liza and an empty chair that presumably was Steve's. Margaret sat next to Henry, who had a smug smile on his face. He winked my way, and I couldn't help but smile back toward him. I'd have to tell him later how much I appreciated his open-mindedness toward me.

There was the sound of microphone tapping and testing, and then the mayor of Ugly Creek, a tall, strong-shouldered man by the name of Gene Stump, was introduced and stepped up to the microphone. "Ladies and gentlemen, we are here tonight to honor the memory of a brave man who gave generously to this community his entire life. A man whose last breath was taken while rescuing victims of the fire that destroyed the gym whose replacement we're in right now."

I heard a soft sob, and saw Maddie's chin trembling. Jake took my hand in his, and I glanced into a face pulled tight with painful remembrance.

"Virgil Clark was not only brave," the speaker

continued, "he was also a hard worker and generous with his time. Many of us learned to play softball from Mr. Clark. He not only coached a team, he took time to personally coach any kid, like me, who was having trouble. He also gave his time to literacy classes. All this while running Clark Electronics and working as a volunteer fireman. He was an amazing man, and I'm honored to present this plaque to his widow and daughter."

Margaret and Madison went up to the small stage and stood beside the mayor. "What the two of them don't know," the mayor continued, "is that due to the generosity of the local businesspeople, a scholarship fund has been started in Virgil Clark's name to help the children of our past and present volunteer firefighters, to achieve their dreams."

The applause was so loud it hurt my ears, while tears temporally blinded me. Quickly I swiped my eyes.

When I looked back toward the front, Maddie and her mother wiped away tears. They shook hands with the mayor, posed for photos, then brought the plaque back to our table. It was a beautiful polished wooden piece with a shiny brass plate mounted on it. The inscription read, "In memory of Virgil Clark, hero. May your memory inspire others for generations to come."

I swallowed back the sob that rose in my throat. I really wish I could have known this amazing person. I hate to admit this, but I was just a little jealous of Maddie having such a man for a father. Unlike mine, who took off without a second thought. Or my stepfather, who thought he was God's gift to Crooked Hollow.

"Another person has requested to speak tonight,"

The mayor said. "I'd like to turn the microphone over to Steve Zapata."

Steve walked up to the podium, and I watched as he stood behind the microphone. He kept licking his lips, and his face was a touch pale. So Zapata wasn't fond of public speaking. I could relate. He looked into the crowd, took a deep breath, and began.

"A great disservice has been done to one among us." He held up a copy of the *Tattler*, and a rumble moved through the crowd. I was suddenly aware a huge hunk of the folks in that room had turned to look my way. Peachy. Just frigging peachy.

"I want to assure you our visitor, Ms. Stephanova, did not, I repeat, *did not*, send this photo to this or any other media."

There was an even louder rumble than before, and one voice shouted out over the rest, "She's a traitor to our town!"

There was a rustle of agreement.

"She's trying to discredit us," another voice yelled.

"No," Steve spoke firmly, though softly enough to capture the attention of the crowd. "She isn't. That's what I'm trying to tell you. This picture is not real and was not sent by Ms. Stephanova. I've checked her computer, and can state definitely that the manufactured photo was sent from an iPhone that does not belong to her."

"It was sent from my iPhone."

I gasped at the voice, as Brandon stepped out onto the stage beside Steve. My brother held up his phone, a grim expression on his face.

"My name is Brandon, and I've held a grudge against my sister Stephie, Ms. Stephanova, for years. I hung on to my hard feelings for so long I forgot what it was I was angry about. A couple of days ago, Butch Johnson and I broke into Margaret Clark's house to check my sister's computer." There was a mass intake of breath followed by the rumbling of murmured conversation. He waited until it quieted somewhat before he continued. "Johnson convinced me that I would find something on there I could use to incriminate or embarrass her. I know my sister pretty well, so it wasn't hard to figure out how to get into her computer. "

I saw him swallow.

"I didn't realize Butch had his own agenda. When we didn't find anything on her computer, he talked me into using a picture Stephie had taken and Photoshopping a hairy creature onto it. Then I sent the fake photo and a fake interview to *The Weekly Tattler*." He indicated the copy he held. "I wanted to hurt my sister, but when she was hurt, I realized how selfish I'd been and turned myself in. I apologize for all the problems I've caused. And I thank Mrs. Clark from the bottom of my heart for not pressing charges."

Cameras flashed all around as Brandon stepped down and disappeared toward the back of the gym.

Steve stepped back to the microphone. "I'd like to ask this be put behind us so we can get back to the real reason for this gathering. I think we'll all agree, what that young man just did is an excellent example of what we came here to honor: heroism."

With that, Steve stepped down. Ignoring questions and comments, he walked to our table and sat beside his wife.

I leaned close to Jake. "He lied. That picture was

real. Won't he get in trouble?"

Jake shook his head. "No, I promise he won't." He squeezed my hand. "Quit worrying and relax. Everything is going to work out."

Slowly I realized the looks I was getting now were friendlier. Smiles replaced the glares. Some people seemed uncomfortable looking toward me, but all in all, things began to relax. Maybe it was my imagination, but I almost began to feel acceptance taking root around me.

I felt a hand on my shoulder and turned to see Aunt Octavia standing behind me. "I told you we take care of our own here." She smiled, gave my shoulder a squeeze, and turned away.

My head was spinning, and I didn't know quite how to deal with it all.

There was food and socializing, and I enjoyed myself more than I would have imagined. Before long, Jake leaned close and whispered, "Don't wear yourself out too much, we still have the Dyami party tomorrow."

"The *what*?"

"Dyami is what the furry guys call their species."

"There's a party? And I'm invited?"

"Yes and yes." He grinned my way, and I realized I couldn't imagine life without him.

"We need to talk," I said.

He nodded, but I saw a little cloud of worry in his dark eyes.

"Don't you trust me?" I whispered.

"With my life," he whispered back.

I hoped I was worthy of his faith.

Chapter 18

Two hours later, we sat on Jake's couch and sipped Coke. He was looking at me with a frown and I could see his chest heaving in rapid breathing. "What's on your mind?"

"Jake. There's a reason I'm nervous about commitment."

"Let me guess, you're really Reese Witherspoon and you have a husband back in Alabama?" He smiled, but the worry in his eyes gave lie to the joke.

"Nothing like that. It's about my family."

"Tell me, sweetheart."

My heart reached for him, and it was all I could do to keep my thoughts straight enough to say what needed saying. "My dad left us when I was five and Mom was still pregnant with Brandon. He just took off and we never knew what happened. Mom hired a private investigator, but he and the cops said the same thing, that he didn't want to be found." I paused to swallow back the pain filling my throat.

"I hate to say this, but are you certain there was no foul play?"

I sucked in the breath I needed to speak again. "I don't know the specifics, but Mom was convinced there wasn't. She seemed so certain I never thought to look into it myself." I stopped to wipe at the tears trying to escape my tightly held control.

"If you want, I know an excellent PI. I'd be happy to talk to him."

"Let me think about it. Please."

Jake brushed back an errant strand of hair. "Whatever you want, honey."

I took a moment to get myself together for the rest. "Not long after Brandon was born Mom met a man, William Donaldson. Before I realized what was happening, Mom was engaged to William. We had to call him that, William. Not Bill or Will or Willie, or whatever. Always William. He said it was to teach us respect." I turned away from Jake, not sure I could continue with the story.

"Tell me," he said, his hand gently rubbing my back.

"He was big on the respect thing. And the discipline thing. He made it clear he thought Mom had let us run wild and he set out to 'tame' us." I took another moment to allow the hatred I felt for the man to rise and then die down enough I could speak.

"He took that 'spare the rod and spoil the child' thing to the max. He used any excuse to hit me or Brandon. I tried to tell Mom, but she wouldn't listen. I don't know if she just chose to ignore what was in front of her, or if he convinced her we were so bad we needed violent treatment to keep us in line. The worst wasn't the beatings, though. The worst was him saying over and over and over we'd never amount to anything. That we couldn't be successful because we had our father's blood in our veins."

I looked into Jake's horrified eyes. "That's why I worked so hard to make good grades, to go to Columbia, to land a job at a D.C. magazine. I wanted to show him I was somebody."

"You *are* somebody, honey. You are a very, very special lady, not to mention one hell of a photographer." He pulled me close. "Look, Margaret can manage the store from here. Maybe I'll even sell the place. There's got to be something I can do in D.C."

"You'd never be happy there." I put a hand against Jake's cheek, luxuriating in the roughness of his five o'clock shadow. "The truth is I hate D.C. and I never liked that job. I took it to prove I could, but I don't care anymore what my mom or stepdad thinks. I didn't realize how much I missed small town life until I came here."

A smile began to pull at Jake's sexy, yummy lips. "So, you think you might be happy in a town called Ugly Creek?"

I felt my own smile grow on my face. "I'm beginning to think this is the only place I *could* be happy. I love this town. And I love you."

He pulled me close and we spent time doing some good old-fashioned necking. Then, we went to bed and did even more.

****

By noon the next day, most of the town was gathered in a clearing in the middle of nowhere. The woods were thick around us, we'd had to walk more than a mile to get there—though four-wheelers were used for those who couldn't make the trip and for some of the bulkier supplies. "The entire area will be cleaned up later," Jake told me. "The cleaners know what they're doing, too. It'll be impossible to know this event took place here."

I settled back in one of the lawn chairs we'd

brought with us. "Do the Bigfeet...I mean the Dyami, live near here?"

Jake sat in the other chair and stretched out his long legs. "No, they live in caves you wouldn't see the entrance to if you were right in front of one."

"No wonder they've never been proven to exist."

He grinned. "It's a real conspiracy."

I wasn't in such a lighthearted mood. "I almost blew the whole thing wide open."

"Not you."

"Brandon." I picked a bit of lint off my shorts. "Using a photo I took. I used personal info to lock the computer and the file, something not recommended."

Jake squeezed my hand. "You took a picture of something amazing. You locked it on your laptop. You couldn't have known your brother would break into your computer. "

"I still feel bad about the whole thing."

"That caring heart of yours is why I love you." That expression, the one he had on his face as he leaned in to kiss me. Wow! I was one lucky woman.

"Would you like some iced tea?" he asked.

"Sure." I watched him go toward the long table, covered with food and drinks. Handsome, well-built, a rear that could inspire poetry. Yum.

"I told you that you belonged here."

I turned to smile at Aunt Octavia. She was dressed in a pink jogging outfit, and was barefoot. I started to ask what that was about, but before I could, she spoke, "I have a message from your father."

I swallowed hard. All of a sudden I understood what made Jake uncomfortable with Auntie's messages. "Is he dead?" I asked.

"Yes, he has passed beyond our plane of existence," she said. "But don't mourn him. His only regret was he couldn't be there for his children. He wishes a wonderful life for you, and hopes soon his son will also find happiness."

I felt a touch on my shoulder and turned to see Brandon standing beside me. "I'm really sorry, sis."

I popped out of the chair and grabbed him with everything I was worth, convinced that as soon as I touched him he'd back away, but instead he pulled me into a warm, snug, welcome hug. "I missed you," I told him.

"I missed you too." He gave me a little breathing room, and I looked up into red, tear-filled eyes. "I was such an idiot," he said.

"I'm sorry I left you with him."

"You couldn't take me with you." He swiped at his wet face. "I knew that when you left, but I resented you for leaving me anyway. I'm just glad you got out of there."

"I love you, Brandon. It almost killed me to leave my little brother with that monster, but I thought I had to go to Columbia. I thought I had to show him I could be somebody."

"I'm proud of you, sis. I'm proud of your good grades, that you went to Columbia, that you have a great job. I always knew you were an amazing photographer, now the world knows too."

I swallowed. "Um, Brandon, I'm not going back to D.C. I'm going to stay here in Ugly Creek."

A slow smile pulled at Brandon's lips, revealing that cute dimple in his right cheek, the one the girls always went crazy over. "It's that guy isn't it? That

Jake guy Butch is so crazy jealous of."

"Jake's definitely part of the reason, but there are others. Like how much I hate living in a big city. And how I actually miss small town life. Do you believe it?"

"Yeah, I do." He looked around him. "Besides, this place is really special. There's something different here."

"Besides the Bigfoot family?"

He laughed, and the sound spilled through me like a cold glass of lemonade on a hot summer day. "It's been years since I've heard you laugh," I said.

"You'll hear it more, because I intend to keep in contact with you this time."

"Why didn't you return my calls?"

He looked down, chewing on his bottom lip as he did. "William convinced me you didn't care about me."

White-hot fury impaled me. "I'll kill that son of a monkey butt's flea!"

My tall, handsome little brother put a steadying hand on my shoulder. "He's not worth it, sis."

I took a long, deep breath. He was right. Murder, as nice as the thought might be, was not the answer.

Suddenly I remembered my manners. "Brandon, this is…" I turned to see nothing but foliage. "Where did she go?"

I heard footsteps and realized Jake had just walked up. He had three glasses of cold iced tea. He handed me one then held out the second to Brandon. "We haven't actually been introduced. I'm Jake Blackwood."

Brandon took the glass and held out his other hand to shake Jake's. "I'm sure you know I'm Brandon, Buff…*Stephie*'s brother."

"Nice to meet you."

"Jake, have you seen Aunt Octavia?"

He shook his head. "She's not here today. She told Margaret she was going to an out-of-body workshop in Nashville."

I stared at him, wondering if I was honestly losing my mind. Thankfully, Jake didn't notice, he'd already turned to Brandon. "I'll bet you have some interesting stories of Stephie as a kid."

Brandon grinned. "Oh, yeah."

I groaned, but the truth was I was so dang glad to have my little brother back in my life I didn't much care what he told Jake.

"You bad man," a husky voice said. "Ms. Margaret home. You went."

We all turned to find the little Bigfoot…um Dyami behind Brandon.

"You're right," Brandon said to the little guy, who came up to Brandon's shoulder. "It was wrong of me to go into her house without permission. I told her I'm sorry, and she asked me to help her with some things to make up for what I did."

"He's not a bad man, Abukcheech," Jake said. "He did a bad thing because someone convinced him it was the right thing to do."

The little creature scrunched up his leathery forehead. "Not bad?"

"No, he just did a bad thing."

"I take doll. Cousin cry."

I saw Jake's lips quirk, but he held on to his stern expression. "That's right. You aren't a bad person, but that wasn't a nice thing to do. Was it?"

"No." The little creature looked down for a minute, then toward Brandon. "Baseball. I learn?"

"I would love to teach you."

Brandon and the little Bigfoot took off toward a cleared and flattened area.

I glanced toward the house and saw Margaret and a Bigfoot talking together. Surprisingly, the Bigfoot, I mean Dyami, had on a dress. "They wear clothes?"

"Mostly for the sake of humans. They think it's strange we're so easily embarrassed," Jake said. "Besides, in the forest it would be too easy to spot them."

I studied the dress-wearing creature and realized it had much more delicate features than either of the other Dyami I'd seen.

"That's Chepi, Nootau's wife."

To one side, the Bigfoot who'd had a gun held on him—Nootau—was talking and laughing with some of the men from town. He caught sight of Chepi and went over to her. He kissed her on the ear, and she turned and smiled at him. I saw the look in their eyes, the look of true love, of forever after.

"Surreal," I whispered.

"Think you could live in a surreal world?"

I smiled. "I'm not sure I could live in the regular world. Not anymore."

I caught a glimpse of movement in the trees to my left and turned that way. A tiny creature stepped into view, about three feet high, gray skin, huge eyes and a small slit for a mouth. I instinctually reached for my camera, but in mid-motion I thought better of it and waved toward the critter instead. It waved back, then as quickly as it appeared it disappeared into the woods.

"Good choice," Jake said.

I smiled. "I'm learning."

He ran a fingertip down my cheek. "Good, because I want you here with me."

"I seem to have fallen in love with both a man and a town."

Then I was in his arms and he was kissing me like I'd never been kissed before. When we came up for air, I looked deep into his eyes. "There are some things I need to take care of first. Things back home in Alabama."

"What do you think your folks will think of me?"

I felt happiness wash over me. "I don't really care. They're stuck with you whether they like it or not. For a long, long, long time."

Jake chuckled as he pulled me close again.

"Get a room," Maddie's voice called.

"Later," Jake whispered. And I smiled with anticipation.